HOLD-UP AT HONDO BEND

Men were getting killed and soldiers were not getting their pay because of the raids by the bandits. Bandido Vicente Tularez had been assured by the deputy that the pay-wagon would only have an escort of no more than six armed troopers. He had reckoned without Lieutenant Phil Crockett of Fort Yuma and his band of troops from the crack 'C' Troop.

H.R

For Alan and Sue Ladd, not forgetting
David, Alana, Carol Lee and Laddie.

Dales Large Print Books
Long Preston, North Yorkshire,
BD23 4ND, England.

British Library Cataloguing in Publication Data.

Stuart, Logan
  Hold-up at Hondo Bend.

    A catalogue record of this book is
    available from the British Library

    ISBN   1-84262-117-3 pbk

First published in Great Britain in 1954 by Rich & Cowan

Cover illustration © A Lloyd Jones by arrangement with
Allied Artists

The moral right of the author has been asserted

Published in Large Print 2002 by arrangement with
Roxy Bellamy, care of Watson, Little Ltd.

Dales Large Print is an imprint of Library Magna Books Ltd.

Printed and bound in Great Britain by
T.J. (International) Ltd., Cornwall, PL28 8RW

CONTENTS

CHAPTER 1

A HELL OF A START!

He lay full-length, belly down, in the inky shadows cast by the 'dobe wall which ran on into utter darkness a few feet behind him.

Rivulets of blood ran down his back and legs; already the whipcord trousers were assuming a stickiness which made the cavalryman wonder whether he were not more badly wounded than he had figured.

His thoughts at this moment were harsh with self-condemnation and he winced every so often at the way he had allowed his enthusiasm to supersede the caution which should always, with wise courage, predominate in a lieutenant's make-up.

This angry self-recrimination caused even more pain than the buck-shot wounds which his back and legs had taken, though partially in glancing fashion.

If that fool with the scatter-gun had been twenty yards closer, Lieutenant Phil Crockett of Fort Yuma would have been a dead pigeon!

It was this thought which rankled, coupled with the fact that even before Phil had gotten going on his self-appointed chore, he had slipped badly, like any raw recruit.

But for the fact that the shot-gun hombre had had his attention distracted by further shouts from the Bank, at the very moment he had blasted away, he would probably have seen his quarry fall and would have followed up with a quick search there and then.

As it was, the lawman (Crockett figured him to be the sheriff or deputy) had been called urgently and during that brief respite Phil Crockett had dragged his long, raw-boned frame from the narrow shadows in front of the board-walk, to this deeper wider patch of black, farther back near the long, high 'dobe wall.

If lady luck had been mean in letting Phil get sprayed with small shot and twisting his ankle as he fell, she had it in mind to make amends, contrariwise, her first step being that Web Skogee, the deputy with the shot-gun, had been forced to answer Sheriff Frank Peck's frantic call for help, without even being sure that he had downed one of the Bank robbers with his shot-gun.

Crockett had started to get to his feet, un-mindful of the townsfolk hurrying along the board-walks. As far as they were concerned, they probably figured he was reeling drunk and had just been thrown out of Maria Cordoba's 'El Cuchillo,' the name she gave her cantiña with its broad sweep of a bar-room and its roulette, monte and faro layout.

Again Phil Crockett thought, *this is a hell of a start,* and painfully proceeded to try crawling along the 'dobe wall in the very faint hopes of reaching a door or archway which might lead into the patio at the rear of the cantiña.

There was still quite a din, though faint at this distance, coming from the 'dobe-walled Bank which the bandits had evidently robbed, though how successfully, Phil Crockett had no means of knowing.

Only a few minutes ago, it seemed, in all probability no more than a quarter hour, he had been an innocent onlooker, having stabled the big army gelding at the livery and then strolling down the main street of 'dobe and clap-board buildings, giving this small township of Hondo Bend his first real and careful scrutiny.

Then with shocking suddenness a dull booming sound had reached his ears. Subconsciously he had noted the lights behind the batwing doors of the cantiña a hundred yards or so up the street and had made out the painted sign in the light cast from the chrome-filled windows. El Cuchillo, the knife! Then the muffled explosion had sounded and men's voices joined in excitedly, talking together in Spanish and Americano.

Phil Crockett had instinctively sprung forward to offer his assistance, his gun, if need be, in the service of law and order and as he had crossed the street at a dead run, a black-shaded silhouette against the town's lights, a man's voice had bellowed out and a shotgun had blasted him, gouging and pebbling his back and legs with the small but deadly shot! He had half-fallen, half-run into the shadows of the board-walk thrown out across the dusty street, and had fetched up with a shattering jolt against the wooden platform itself.

There, for a moment, he had been invisible in the dark cast shadows and then the lawman had been called back...

Now Phil Crockett crawled painfully through the dust on hands and knees, dragging the more badly damaged left leg stiffly behind him. There was just a slim chance, he told himself, and then his groping fingers felt the wrought iron-work of a gate, set in the baked mud wall. He sent up a quick, earnest prayer that the gate should be unlocked and pushed with all the strength called up from his draining reserves. He figured he must be more bad hurt than he had at first thought. He felt sick with the effort of crawling and pushing and almost too tired to ease himself through into the hard-packed earth compound beyond the now open gate.

He could see the velvety blackness of the sky as he looked up and thought for a moment that lights were dancing before his eyes until he grinned meagrely, realizing that the night sky was sprinkled with a myriad of stars, and away to the east a lazy sickle moon swung over this mañana-land wherein Hondo Bend was situated.

He propped himself up on one arm and with his free hand wiped some of the sweat and dust from his face. He heard the renewed sounds of men's voices, nearer now, raised in unbridled anger and inflected with the unchecked run of desires and primitive emotions, rather than with a cool detachment.

C Troop, Phil told himself bleakly, would run an outlaw down, even an Apache buck, without letting their blood lust get the better of them; such was army discipline and schooling. A civilian pack, however mild-mannered, seemed to run amuck at the first sign of a cornered gunman, revelling almost in a brutality which could aptly be measured by way of contrast through their milk-and-water attitudes in more peaceful situations.

But another sound had reached Crockett's keen ears, even as his head hung down and his senses began to swim. He fought the nausea which threatened him and turned his head towards the loggia at back of which he dimly realized was El Cuchillo.

A door had opened only a few feet away and bright light stabbed out into the darkness, spilling across the patio and bracketing the hard-breathing, blood-stained figure on the ground.

Phil shook his head and some of the sweat and mists seemed to clear from his dark grey eyes for a moment, so that he saw the woman clearly, standing by the open door gazing down at him, pity and horror emanating from the black depths of her velvety eyes...

He seemed to be losing consciousness, and that at a time when he needed all his faculties and the ability to think clearly. But somehow he didn't care. It didn't seem to matter and then, strangely, his mind was suddenly clear and the mental images conjured up by his thoughts were para-doxically no longer vague and nebulous but clear-cut and sharply silhouetted...

He was standing rigidly to attention in front of his own commanding officer. Major Blaine Mitchell gave his kindly smile reserved for such occasions as this when he was interviewing Lieutenant Phil Crockett whom he had known since C Troop's senior lieutenant had been a boy trumpeter.

'At ease, Phil,' Blaine Mitchell said. 'Take a pew and rest your legs!'

Crockett's smile was fleeting as he straddled a hard-wood chair; yet there was that in both men's expressions which held a bleak reserve as though the smile were merely a momentary courtesy, not a gesture or expression of humour.

Perhaps Crockett, more than anyone else at Fort Yuma, had reason to feel tight and revengeful inside, since the news of the attack by bandidos on the army paymaster's wagon and the really bitter, tragic information that Lieutenant Cass Cherry, the officer in charge of the small escort, had been killed.

Cass Cherry had been Crockett's particular friend. Off-duty they had ridden together; visited the Mex villages and American towns and had drunk their tequilla together when rye was not to be had.

There had been but five troopers in the detail, with Lieutenant Cherry in charge and Paymaster Clinton Wickler on the wagon seat alongside the driver. There had been no special reason to regard this as anything other than the normal monthly journey from Phoenix. But bandidos had struck quickly and cunningly, throwing the small escort into confusion by the very force and suddenness of their concentrated attack.

There had been a veritable hail of lead

from both sides the trail; a withering cross-fire which sent the troopers down before sun-blackened hands could drag the Springfields from saddle-boots.

The wounded had been completely ignored by the masked riders except for one who kept his carbine trained on the now swearing, helpless men. Cass Cherry was a still, bloody figure, sprawled grotesquely across the wagon-trees. Clinton Wickler was barely conscious and Ed Travers, like Lieutenant Cherry, would ride no more.

It was so easy the way the bandidos helped themselves to the box of bills and silver and gold pieces and quickly divided it up, thrusting the money into flour sacks which were immediately thrown across the horns of the high, double-rigged Mex saddles.

Two wounded troopers essayed shots at the disappearing bandits, but had no way of knowing where their bullets had gone. In a few minutes only, the scene was quiet except for the shrill scream of the offside wagon horse and the low groans and softly breathed curses of the wounded and the slowly settling alkali dust.

It had been a sorry, bloody cavalcade that had finally found its way back to Fort Yuma minus nearly three thousand dollars' pay for nine hundred officers and men. But the worst of it, even to the most devil-may-care of the gambling raw-boned Irish Troopers, had not been the loss of the dinero. They would get their pay eventually anyway. It had been the deaths of Cass Cherry and Ed Travers the driver, which had affected the Fort most of all, and particularly had it stirred Lieutenant Phil Crockett.

'You know that both Yuma and the territorial capital have sent men and have picked up nothing fresh on the business last week, Phil. Was it about that you wanted to see me?'

Crockett nodded and at an encouraging sign from Mitchell built himself a cigarette.

'I guess we've all realized for a long time, sir,' Crockett said, 'that this is just about the last outpost of civilization as far as Washington is concerned. Neither can we expect much help from the Governor's men or individual marshals and sheriffs–'

Blaine Mitchell nodded and tugged at his iron-grey dragoon moustaches. 'You got anything in mind, Phil?'

Crockett shifted restlessly across the chair, marshalling his thoughts and then coming straight to the point.

'I want to go out and get a line on these greaser devils, Major, if you'll let me. We know for sure it was Vicente's band. Wickler and two of the men identified that bunch as Mexes and no other outlaw gang besides Vicente Tularez' has as many men. Pols Freyer reckoned there was up to a dozen

15

riders all wearing chihuahua hats, cross bandaleros, knives and all the rest. The usual walking arsenals of the greaser bandidos.

'I don't want or expect any help from the fort, Major,' Crockett continued. 'Once I leave here on an unbranded gelding, rigged out as a foot-loose cowpoke riding the chucklines, I'll be on my own–'

'You've got it figured out as far as that?' Blaine Mitchell's brows when up but there was a hint of admiration in his blue eyes.

'The hold-up was at Hondo Bend,' Phil Crockett continued. 'My plan is to trail from there along the river to the town of that name. I'll have to dig myself in somehow and find out whatever I can. I've got a hunch that Hondo Bend might prove to be the hub of the whole thing.'

'What do we know about the Tularez gang?' Blaine Mitchell asked cautiously.

'We know, or at least we're pretty sure, that after each hold-up – bank, prospector – whatever it might be, Vicente lights out for some hidey-hole in the Eagle Tail mountains. We know, more or less, how they dress – they're not peons though they are murderers and robbers a dozen times over. Give me a chance, Major, to find out more; to point the finger at that goddam bunch and not only revenge Cass Cherry but perhaps help to recover the pay-roll – or some

16

of it at least!'

'If you were to do this, Phil,' Mitchell answered, 'it would have to be kept mighty quiet. If either Washington or Prescott got to hear about a U.S. Cavalry lieutenant playing lawman-detective, there'd be hell to pay. Our job is to protect whites, fight Indians and bandits, yes, but not send first-class officers out as spies to winkle out ruthless gangs singlehanded.'

'I guess I wouldn't be able to tackle them singlehanded anyway, Major. My idea is to get more information about Tularez and his band; find out some of their habits and even, if possible, where they are likely to strike next. We might even spring a trap for them by *encouraging them to attack* the next thinly escorted paymaster's wagon...'

Crockett allowed his suggestion to run on, knowing that in the following silence, Blaine Mitchell was chewing on the idea.

The major's glance lifted presently to Crockett's lean, sunburned face. He said: 'A drifting cowpoke on an unbranded gelding. A Winchester instead of a Springfield, a soogan roll instead of army blankets; a Walker six instead of a Navy Colt. Yes, it might be done, Phil, if there's some way of keeping me posted and calling on us for help when you're ready? You're not known in Hondo Bend?'

Phil Crockett shook his head. 'Mostly on

17

leave we've visited Mohawk, Gila, Maricopa Wells and Phoenix. I guess we haven't been through Hondo Bend above a couple of times.' He said 'we' because he still thought of Cass Cherry as his saddle-partner. It was painfully difficult to realize that he was gone…

'Do you figure on enlisting the law's help in Hondo Bend?'

'I'd have to wait and see first, sir. It's not impossible that the law is crooked or even in cahoots with Vicente's bunch. It wouldn't be the first time.'

Crockett raised his head with an effort and wondered whether he had been dreaming. Yet he could not have lost consciousness for more than a few seconds, he thought. The woman was still standing in the flagged loggia just in front of the half-open door.

She spoke now, for the first time, the richness of her low voice overlaying the actual spoken words.

'You are hurt, señor,' she said slowly. 'Ees much blood–' she broke off suddenly and called something in Spanish through the half-open door at her back. Crockett heard the name 'Esteban' and made a try for the six-gun at his hip, at the same time essaying to rise unsteadily to his feet. He stood there, swaying groggily, favouring the left ankle which was badly swollen and feeling the dull ache in his back and the stickiness of half-dried blood on his legs.

A small, wiry looking little Mex came in answer to the woman's low-voiced, urgent summons. He had a kerchief tied round his grey head and a face like a wrinkled walnut. Across his thin body he wore a shirt and short, bolero jacket, and the wiry legs were encased in tight velvet trousers with flared bottoms. He gazed at Crockett with his black, unwinking stare and presently shuttled his glance back to the woman.

'The loft, Estaban, quickly,' she said in Spanish and Crockett's hand dropped from his gun as Estaban darted forward with surprising agility, putting an arm round the sagging blood-stained figure and whispering fiercely into his ear.

'We 'elp you, señor. Try to walk, si?'

He commenced moving towards a collection of outbuildings half-supporting Crockett's dragging body with amazing strength. The woman went on ahead, leading the way to a stable, dimly lit by a hanging lantern.

'Into the loft, Estaban, and hurry,' she said, indicating the ladder pointing upwards to the hay-loft. She turned to Crockett and spoke in her broken English.

'Please 'elp, señor, an' try to climb eento the loft. The sheriff 'e come queeckly now.'

Crockett nodded, wondering dimly why these people should be helping him at all.

19

He had his brief but clear view of the woman's face as she came within radius of the hanging lantern. He saw the faintest shade of olive in the beautifully boned face, underneath the madder tinge of her cheeks. The eyes were large and dark, but not black as he had first thought, rather a deep, violet-blue with thick black lashes fringing them. He mentally chided himself for wasting time as colour slowly rode the marble column of her throat.

'Gracias, señorita,' he murmured and girded himself for the task of mounting the ladder...

Estaban caught up a last handful of hay, placing it carefully on top of Crockett's almost completely covered body.

'Stay quiet, señor, until thees sheriff hombre he ees gone! You sabe?'

Crockett nodded and managed a weak grin. 'Gracias, Estaban,' he said as the little man turned and descended the ladder, closing the trap-door behind him...

CHAPTER 2

EL CUCHILLO

His first thought on waking was that he had dozed off for a few minutes. He listened carefully but could hear no sounds at first that would give him any indication of time, or what was happening outside.

Then, quite near at hand and with startling clearness, a rooster crowed. Through a chink in the 'dobe building, Crockett fancied he could see the merest sliver of light in the dark sky, over to the east.

He moved his body and at once felt the tight pressage of bandages around his back and legs. The pain, which before had been fierce as a flame, was now only a dull throbbing ache.

He knew then that he had slept deeply; that dawn was near at hand and that either Esteban, *or the woman,* had dressed his wounds whilst he had slept the deep sleep of mental and physical exhaustion.

He felt his cheeks go hot in the sweet-smelling, dark interior of the hay-loft. Then Crockett shrugged and managed a wry grin, gradually achieving a sitting-up position without too much pain or discomfort.

He fished in his pocket for papers and built a smoke, carefully shoving the stacked up hay to one side and extinguishing the sulphur match between thumb and forefinger.

He smoked gratefully, enjoying the tang of tobacco on his tongue and the sharpness of the smoke as he expelled it from his nostrils. Gratitude was a strong thing in him, not merely for the solace of a cigarette but because an unknown Mex (or Spanish?) woman and a little wizened Mex mozo had helped him last night. He remembered the story of the Good Samaritan way back from his school days. After all, who was he to be helped and nursed and hidden by complete strangers? He, a complete stranger himself, a gringo to boot!

He did not find it difficult to conjure up a picture of the woman as he recollected her last night, bathed in the soft yellow light from the lantern.

He could see the blue-black sheen of her hair as inky as a raven's wing and the soft smoothness of her cheeks and the red generous curve of her lips.

He remembered she had worn some kind of gown, tight-waisted and flowing to her feet, which had yet shown off the curves of her supple figure and had contrasted vividly with the creamy pallor of her neck and throat...

He turned his head and put his face to the chink in the wall which was now showing a brighter gleam of light. Somewhere off, he heard the soft but gradually ascending sounds of a household awakening.

Footfalls echoed sharply across the flagged patio and then softened as boots hit the hard-packed earth.

Crockett drew his gun and spun the cylinder, examining each load in turn. He waited, gun in hand, determined now to fight his way out if the need arose.

But there seemed to be only one person ascending the ladder and Phil was not surprised when he heard Esteban's low voice from the other side of the trap-door.

'Do not shoot, Señor Americano, eet ees Esteban weeth food for you!'

Phil grinned and re-sheathed his gun, reaching forward to ease the flap back as Esteban's wizened face appeared.

In one hand the little Mex was miraculously balancing a tray on which were set a plate of hot tortillas and a carafe of water, as well as a jug of tequila.

'Señorita Cordoba weesh me to say buenos dias for her, señor, an' tell you to eat food goddam queeck!' As he spoke, Esteban set down the tray and squatted back on his bootheels as though he intended to make himself generally responsible for the señor eating his breakfast.

But he need not have worried. In spite of the buck-shot wounds and the now eased throbbing in back and legs, Phil Crockett proceeded to do ample justice to Señorita Cordoba's fare, hot as the tortillas were.

Several times Crockett had to rinse his mouth with the cool spring water in the carafe.

Presently he asked a question, speaking in Spanish, much to Esteban's obvious surprise and pleasure.

'The Señor Americano speeks the mother tongue like a true Mexican,' he grinned.

'You're not so bad yourself, Esteban, when it comes to Americano!'

Esteban chuckled and then became serious. 'Si, señor,' he replied, 'the shereef an' deputy come lookin' for someone at El Cuchillo. But *we* don' know 'oo they look for. Por Dios! They say they look for Mejicano bandido – one 'oo 'elped rob the bank las' night. Señorita Cordoba do not feegure *you* look like Mex bandido so she say "no", she don' know what they goddam talk about! She not sabe! You, Americano! You not Mexican bandido, si?'

'I'm not, Esteban,' Phil said, pushing his now empty plate to one side and pouring out a little of the tequila. 'But some smart alec of a John Law apparently mistook me for one, last night.'

Crockett told his story briefly and then

24

Esteban stood up, catching up the tray and preparing to descend the ladder.

'Ees much like the señorita feegure,' he told Crockett. 'But now you stay steel. I come back soon an' maybe you can wash.'

Maria de Mendoza y Cordoba (to give her the full name by which her Castillian family had been known in that part of Mexico which later became California), stood in the gloomy entrance of Hondo Bend's feed-barn and livery stable, searching the soft, lamp-lit shadows ahead with her dark, bright gaze.

Maria Cordoba was a woman whose mental ability and determination had been sired by adversity. The only daughter of Don Juan de Mendoza y Cordoba, rich land-owner and controller of a vast estancia, and a wonderfully fashioned and furnished casa, Maria had early learned that greed and avarice were quickly spawned from dis-content and overwheening and ruthless ambition. Add to those traits, fierce national and local fanaticism and tragedy, misery and suffering are the inevitable con-sequences.

Thus, the Mexican wars and guerilla actions had stripped the Don of every material possession, including even his beloved wife. Too old, too embittered and too weary to fight on any longer, Don Juan de Mendoza y Cordoba had almost thankfully commended his soul to heaven, leaving his rebellious and fiery young daughter to live as best she could in the care of duenna Isobel and the mozo Esteban.

But after a time, the duenna too passed away, and suddenly, sickened by death and suffering and poverty, Maria had decided to seek fresh fields. Esteban could go with her or not, just as he wished.

But Esteban *had* wished to travel with and look after the lovely young mistress whom he adored and gradually there grew to exist a bond between them which was out of all proportion to their respective stations in life. Here was a camaraderie, an affinity more democratic than any state democracy. And if Maria treated Esteban more as a trusted elder brother, he in turn guarded her jealously and fanatically on the long journey to Sonora and thence, eventually, into the new territory of Arizona.

Many times during the long months of travelling and afterwards, Maria had wished that she was an ugly old hag, with her eyes dull and skin yellow and wrinkled like ancient parchment. For what better way than this, to prevent men, both Americanos and greasers from leering at her, stripping her with their eyes and even trying to make love to her? But that had been years ago now, before Esteban's long cuchillo had become stained with so much blood and before Maria herself had learned not only to repulse with freezing scorn and fierce contempt, but also to *encourage,* so that she might be the richer in her experience in the ways and subterfuges of men.

Thus had Maria Cordoba, with the blood of old Castille flowing in her veins, faced up to adversity and fought back with the fierce resilience of steel. True, even now, she was no great señorita landowner; no high-toned Spanish lady for the crowds to bow to and hosts of mozos to jump at her slightest command. She did not want this for, in a modest way, she had made money running this biggest cantiña and gaming house in town. She could afford to buy of the best and if that best were in no way comparable to the dimly remembered standards of her early childhood, what did it matter?

Now the dark haired Mexican-born woman crossed the threshold making for the hostler's dimly lit office beyond the runway. Cal Bellenger was asleep on his rumpled cot, but Maria wasted no time in rousing him, nor did she indulge in any exhibitions of mock modesty as Cal, surprised and red-faced, hurriedly climbed into denim shirt and waist overalls.

'Cal!' Maria said fiercely, scarcely giving the flustered liveryman time to adjust the last button. ''Ave you a strange hoss in here tonight, si? A ponee ridden by an Americano? Pair'aps 'e left eet weet' you earlier las' night? Speek queeckly, Cal, or I do somet'ing we bot' be ver' sorry for. 'As the shereef, the Frank Peeck 'ombre been 'ere an' ask you sometheeng?'

She waited with a mounting impatience while Cal Bellenger scratched his balding head and attempted to collect his scattered wits.

He stared at her, almost defiantly now. 'You woke me up jest to ask a lotta dam' fool questions, Miz Maria—'

She seized him by the shoulders, her long, graceful fingers digging into his thin flesh like the talons of a predatory bird. Maria Cordoba had physical as well as mental strength.

'You eediot, Cal! I no ask dam' fool questions. Eet ees important! Listen,' she breathed with the soft venom of a hissing snake, 'you tell me what I ask, Cal, or—' she broke off and pulled a folded sheet of paper from the garter above her silk-clad knee.

Bellenger blinked, half in surprise, half in admiration at sight of the shapely leg.

She unrolled the paper and thrust it almost savagely beneath the hostler's nose, right in his startled face. He backed away a few steps and dragged his fascinated gaze from Maria's angrily beautiful eyes to the paper she held so threateningly in front of him. He saw the crudely-drawn likeness of himself, not particularly recognizable but then they had the name off pat and the various aliases he had used back in Donna Anna county, New Mexico, in his small-time but slick robberies.

Not that they rated him very high, he realized half-regretfully. A mere $250 was all the sheriff of Lascruces was offering in exchange for the capture of Brad Kelligrew, alias George Bellenger; or any information which would lead to his arrest.

'Do we look for thees hoss, amigo mio?' Maria said softly. Bellenger looked up and smiled, slowly tearing the dodger into little pieces and grinding the fragments into the floor under his boot-heel.

'What now, Miz Maria?'

'I geeve you one more chance,' Maria Cordoba spoke through her clenched white teeth. 'I have two more beels like that one! Shall we look for thees ponee?'

Bellenger nodded mutely and drew a lantern towards him, lighting it before proceeding to the stalls on either side the runway.

He stopped at the second stall, with Maria close at his heels.

'I guess you must mean this black, Miz Maria,' Bellenger said over his shoulder in a humbler tone of voice.

'Looks like an army gelding to me, though

there don't appear to be no brand on either shoulder or rump!'

'That ees the hoss the stranger rode in las' night, Cal?' Maria asked and the hostler nodded. 'What you want for me to do?'

For answer Maria Cordoba took two twenty-dollar gold pieces from the pouch at her waist and thrust them into the hostler's willing grasp.

'Thees dinero will cover the cost of feed an' shelter,' Maria smiled, 'si? I tak' the hoss away an' you nevair see eet, sabe?'

There was a gentle tap on the trap-door, and Phil Crockett, knowing that it was not made by any lawman's hard-bone knuckles, leaned forward, easing the flap back to admit Maria Cordoba.

He half rose from his squatting position, but she waved him down with an imperious gesture as she closed the trap-door, and stood looking down at him.

Earlier, Crockett had found the two shutters which covered the unglazed window and these were now open to the morning sun and air.

'How you feel thees mornin', señor?' the woman asked. 'Not so bad you could not eat Manuela's tortillas, huh?' She smiled slowly, giving to her serious face a startling brightness. In the morning light, Crockett thought she looked even more beautiful than she had done by lantern light. Inconsequentially, he thought it was a thing which could be truthfully said of few women.

'Thanks to you, Maria Cordoba,' he said, speaking in English, 'I feel pretty good considering. It seems to me, you or Esteban made a good job of that buckshot!'

'We deeg out the pellets after I geeve you a whiff of chlor'form,' she told him, and Crockett's thick brows rose at this information. This woman – or girl, she couldn't be so old – was sure amazing.

He rolled and lit a cigarette, careful as always with the match and strangely and suddenly embarrassed in the woman's presence.

'Your hoss, eet is here, right below, señor. The 'ostler, 'e weel not talk, I see to that!'

'You sure think of most everything, Miss Cordoba,' Phil smiled. 'I guess I owe you and Esteban more than I can ever repay. Like I told your mozo earlier on, I heard the explosion last night just after I'd put the gelding up at the feed barn. I ran across the street, gun in hand, to see what was doing, figuring I might help in some way, but one of your lawmen was a mite trigger-happy and gave me both barrels. Another twenty yards or so, I guess I'd've been buzzard meat.'

She nodded slowly. 'We found out, eet was Web Skogee, Frank Peck's dep'ty. They come las' night to search but no find un bandido. Esteban, he scrub the bloodstains on the patio.'

'My name's Crockett, Phil Crockett–'

'An' you air a soldado from the Fort Yuma, si?'

Crockett tried hard not to register surprise again at this astounding woman's perception.

'How do you figure that one, Maria?' he smiled.

'Your hoss, eet ees a black gelding of a certain size an' shape. The army ees partic'lar, si, about eet's hoss-flesh. True, there ees no U.S. brand and the carbeen, she ees Winchester–'

Crockett grinned and lifted a hand in mock alarm. 'Don't tell me any more, Maria, my life's history wouldn't bear looking into.' He sobered suddenly, knowing that he would have to tell this Spanish señorita *some* of the truth at least.

'I *am* from Fort Yuma,' Crockett admitted. 'Right now I'm playing the role of detective, which same, it appears to me, you would be a dam' sight better at!'

She smiled but did not speak.

'I'm trying to trace a deserter,' Crockett went on, hoping that he would be forgiven for the lies he was telling. 'Not an ordinary case either, because this man caused the death of some of our men.'

'You theenk thees mal hombre ees, mebbe in Hondo Bend?'

Crockett shook his head. 'Not necessarily. We just figured on this town as a starting-off place. He's sure somewhere around the district, maybe here, maybe north of the Gila over to the Eagle Tails.' He watched her closely as he spoke, but could see no flicker beyond deep interest in her dark blue eyes.

'You were seen only as a shadow las' night,' she said, 'so no one knows who you are, what you look lik'! They do not even know you exist at all. Bueno! You rest up at the 'ouse till your wounds heal, then you vamos at night, before the moon, an' ride *back* eento town nex' morning, si? You are un vaquero, sabe? What they call feedle-foot. You look for a job pairhaps but you not in mucho 'urry. You tak' room in Pedrello's place up the street or else book room here in El Cuchillo.'

Crockett let go his breath in a soundless whistle. Maria Cordoba had sure gotten the whole thing figured out and he could find no fault in her suggestions. Indeed, it was very much as he had already planned. He would have to go out and come back again obviously, so that the townsfolk could see him and regard him as a stranger entering Hondo Bend *for the first time*.

True, he had been here once-twice before with Cass Charry but they had not stayed

33

longer than time enough for a few drinks in a cantiña farther down the street. As for the Mexes and Americanos themselves, it was doubtful whether anyone would recognize him after eighteen months and rigged out as he was.

He climbed to his feet slowly, wincing a little and Maria watched soberly, offering no help, sensing intuitively that this man would prefer it that way.

'One thing, Señor Crockett,' she warned him. 'Do not leave before your wounds an' your foot ees well. Mebbe the shereef an' his dep'ty look for un hombre weeth a limp as well as buckshot een 'ees back, no?'

Phil nodded, feeling his confidence restored now that he was standing on his two feet.

'You're smart as well as beautiful, Miss Cordoba,' he said, and saw the stain of colour mount upwards from her throat. He knew his words were clumsy and that the compliment sounded cheap, but again he misjudged her for Maria had looked into his eyes and had read the sincerity there, behind the banal words.

'They 'ave gone rideeng, Peck an' Skogee, to try and cut sign of the bandidos. Por Dios! I deed not tell you that the bank boss, 'e was keeled when they escaped. That ees why you mus' stay 'ere teel your wounds ees better an' you do not leemp!'

34

CHAPTER 3

CROCKETT TRAILS OUT

It was dusk when the two dust-covered riders drew rein at the rack in front of El Cuchillo and tiredly stepped from leather.

Web Skogee wiped sweat and alkali from his caked face with the black kerchief at his throat and batted dust from leather chaps with the weather-stained stetson.

He was a big man, well muscled and as rock hard as an Irish Trooper. Frank Peck, his superior, was more inclined to fat and found these lengthy rides increasingly painful. He was developing a sizeable paunch which was inclined to sway uncomfortably when he was aboard a jolting horse. But now he heaved a sigh of relief as he tromped across the board-walk and pushed open the batwing doors, Skogee following at his heels.

The long bar at the end of the vast room had its sprinkling of townsfolk and a few waddies from outlying spreads.

El Cuchillo was a swell-looking place, with its whitewashed 'dobe walls hung with gaily coloured ponchos and cuchillos, the latter in beautifully wrought leather scabbards. From the raftered ceiling hung a myriad of bright-reflectored coal-oil lamps. The bar was also something of which Maria Cordoba was justly proud, being an exquisitely polished piece of Californian redwood. One side of the big room was partly occupied by booths and the gambling layout; roulette, monte, faro, chuck-a-luck. There were more chairs and tables the other side of the bar and, at the end, a small flare-lit stage for which from time to time, Maria procured professional dancers and actors.

The finest cantiña and gambling saloon west of the Rio Grande, was Maria's boast and, while all such exaggerated claims were treated with frank incredulity, nevertheless, the statement was perhaps not so far from the truth.

Heads turned in the direction of the lawmen as they crossed to the bar where Jeff the bartender had their usual shot-glasses of whisky ready and waiting.

Maria, with a brief nod to Gonzales, her house-gambler, left the roulette wheel and sauntered across to the bar.

'Welcome, señores, to El Cuchillo. You look tired an' lik' you have 'ad leetle success, si?'

Holt Caddo, mayor of Hondo Bend, wiped his luxuriant moustaches and switched his gaze from Maria to the lawmen.

'That right, Frank? You had no luck trailing those scallawags?'

Frank Peck nodded and downed a half of his drink. He indicated the deputy at his side. 'Web'll tell you we plumb wore out our broncs an' ourselves trailin' them bustards all day, to the Eagle Tails, but as usual, one moment the sign is plain, next, it jest ain't there at-all!'

'This is a bad business, men,' Holt Caddo said. 'Ty Edwards killed and several thousand dollars' dinero lifted.'

'Figger they'd've taken a sight more,' Frank Peck grunted, 'only they hadn't reckoned on the dynamite blastin' away so much an' kickin' up sech a racket. As it was, I got there almost afore the smoke had cleared!'

'Everyone knows you were right on your toes, Frank,' the mayor said generously. 'Web, too. You figure, Web, you hit that one you blasted at?'

Skogee wiped the black longhorn moustaches which bracketed his mouth almost to his square, jutting chin.

'Figger I hit him, Mayor, but evidently not bad enough to stop him. Could've gotten another twen'y yards closer an' we'd have got him sure. As it was he was runnin' at a right smart lick. Reckon the pellets glanced off him, is all!'

'Something's got to be done about these

robberies, Mayor,' the thin faced owner of the mercantile put in. 'It'll be stores an' shops next, you see if it won't, with mebbe folks killed on the walks right here in town!'

'What you suggest they should do, Señor Bexar?' Maria put in. 'Already you see Frank an' Web ride all day after thees bandidos–'

'That's right, Jud,' Holt Caddo interrupted hurriedly, 'we're doing everything we can and don't forget we're not the only ones. Fact is, this is the first time the town's been hit. You recollect a week or two ago, Vicente's band attacked an army detail and got away with Fort Yuma's payroll. Hell! If the army cain't fight them off, how in the heck can you expect *me,* with two lawmen, to bust them up?'

'Reckon we need a few Governor's men down here,' another voice chimed in. 'Me, I had close to five hun'ed dollars stashed in Ty Edwards' safe. Now they say they kin only pay out a half of everyone's balance!'

'We're plumb lucky they didn't have time to swipe the lot, I'd say,' the sheriff murmured, refilling his now empty shot-glass. 'Dammit, George, we ain't no 'Paches to be able to follow a sign that plumb peters out. All right! So we know it was Vicente's gang – at least we're pretty certain. I caught a glimpse of five-six Mexes mounting their broncs, but they was gone in a flash before

I could fire.

'We know, too, Vicente's gotten himself a nice hidey-hole in the Eagle Tails. I tell you, George, and you, Bexar, to trail them bandidos an' dig 'em out from the mountains we'd need an armed posse of a hundred men and even then it'd take more'n a week of Sundays!'

'I'm afraid the sheriff's right, men,' Holt Caddo confirmed. 'All I can do is write to Prescott and ask the Governor again if he can take any further steps about these outlaws. But remember, we're a long way from the capital and there's a good few thousands of square miles – and outlaws – for Prescott to deal with aside from Maricopa and Hondo Bend!'

For the second time within the week, Phil Crockett rode into town. But as far as the townsfolk were concerned he was a drifting cow-poke hitting Hondo Bend for the first time. Everyone believed that without hesitation, except Maria and Esteban and Cal Bellenger and none of them would talk!

Again Crockett put his horse up at Bellenger's livery and neither man so much as batted an eyelid as Phil paid over a generous amount 'for the care of his horse'!

He lit a cigarette and strolled out onto the street, figuring the best move was to make himself immediately known to the law.

His wounds, still bandaged under his shirt, scarcely bothered him and the swollen ankle was almost back to normal. Just so long as he didn't look like a limping gun-shot case, he figured he was safe enough. Not that he would have had much difficulty in proving his innocence; but if he *did* have to do that it would mean referring to the fort and shouting his secret mission from the rooftops. Thus, if anyone in town were in cahoots with Vicente's gang, Tularez himself would be amply warned and prepared!

No! He must go on as he started, making this an entirely solo, undercover affair. If, and when, he was able to get anything on Vicente, then, and then only, would he ask for Major Mitchell's co-operation.

He entered the sheriff's office through the open door and approached the desk.

Frank Peck looked up and regarded the stranger with his mild, incurious gaze.

'Just hit town, Sheriff, and figured you might be able to tell me where I can get a bed and a good meal. Name's Crockett, Pete Crockett–'

'Drifting cowpuncher?'

Phil nodded and Peck's gaze travelled over the tall, raw-boned figure in front of him, from the low-crowned, dust-covered stetson to the scuffed, spurred boots. Neither did Frank's eyes miss the sagging cartridge belt with the walnut-handled six protruding from the worn scabbard. Evidently the stranger was not prepared to give his life history, and after a few moments' silence, the sheriff spoke again.

'You kin get a good bed at Dooley's Rooms and a meal or drink most anyplace in Hondo Bend. If you want all of them things together under one roof, try El Cuchillo across the way.'

'Mex place?' Crockett asked idly.

'Run on Mex lines, mebbe,' Peck said, 'but the Señorita Maria Cordoba who owns the joint ain't no greaser dame. She's pure Spanish from way back or I don't know the difference between a head-band and a breech-clout! You figger on stayin' long?'

Crockett dropped his cigarette butt and ground it out under his boot.

'Got enough dinero to last a week or so,' he told the sheriff. 'Reckon I'll see if any ranch-owners come into town wanting hands.'

Peck rose to his feet and fiddled with the papers on his desk. 'Don't flash your bills around,' he warned, 'we jest done had bank robbers nigh on a week ago. Mex bandidos. Another thing. We don't mind strangers jest so long as they cause no trouble. You want a ridin' job, I daresay Sedge Jones of Pothook or Haskell of Three Feathers'll be into town within a day or two.'

Crockett nodded, turned on his heel and

41

crossed the street to 'The Knife,' Maria's place.

Well, he had shown himself openly to the law and had told his story; now he would sample some more of Maria's whisky, this time in public.

His back muscles quivered as he crossed the dusty street; he recollected the last time he had started across and had run and been cut down with the hornet-stings of sprayed buck-shot.

He pushed at the batwing doors and blinked in the bright lights, moving slowly towards the bar. He glimpsed Maria at the roulette table and imagined he saw relief swim into the dark pools of her eyes.

He joined the men at the bar as their gazes moved over him in silent speculation. 'Whisky,' he told the bartender and caught the quick, solemn wink of Esteban at the farther end of the counter.

The barkeep came back with a fresh bottle of rye and a shot-glass, pushing them across the gleaming bar top. Crockett laid a silver piece alongside and asked about a room.

'Esteban'll fix you up,' Jeff said, indicating the small Mex with a jerk of his head. 'You want a good meal, stranger, the dinin'-room's straight through those drapes!' The main reason that inspired Jeff to exert such efforts of salesmanship as he possessed was that Maria Cordoba paid commission to any of her staff who introduced business. Thus, when Jeff, closely watching the tall stranger, saw him turn presently and walk towards the drapes, he grinned and fished out a slate from under the bar, marking thereon in chalk his own cabalistic symbols which would add to his commission maybe as much as a quarter.

Maria, seeing the covert yet meaningful expression on Jeff's face, smiled to herself and, shortly, followed Crockett through into the restaurant part of the cantiña.

For the benefit of other diners, Maria smiled only in a professional way and then infrequently. But by the time she had 'welcomed' the Americano to El Cuchillo and had beckoned a mozo to execute the stranger's order, the rest of the room had accepted the whole thing as normal practice, knowing from long experience that although Maria served only the best, she also had a good eye open to business.

Several folks eating gave Crockett the benefit of their brief stares and wondered who he might be. One or two were not far wrong when they placed him as an ex-trooper and then turned back to their meals.

Under cover of the general noise of talk, clatter of dishes and scrape of boots, Maria and Phil were able to talk freely.

From back in the saloon a Mex band started up and Phil caught a glimpse of several percentage girls as they passed the drapes on their way to the main room.

'Quite a place you've got, Maria, now I can see it properly.'

She nodded and brushed the compliment aside as of no consequence.

'You got back eento town wit'out trouble, señor? No one suspected?'

He shook his head and smiled at her seriousness.

'I guess I'm just a foot-loose cow-poke,' he told her. 'Even been to the sheriff to put myself square with the law. Incidentally,' Phil went on, leaning forward across the table, 'I gave my name as *Pete* Crockett, so don't go calling me "Pheel".'

This time she smiled, but made no answer as the mozo brought Crockett's meal and Phil, smelling the appetizing Mex-cooked victuals, suddenly realized he was hungry...

An hour after dawn's first light, Crockett emerged from El Cuchillo and lit his first cigarette of the day. He stood on the walk, breathing in the oven-hot air only partially cooled by the nearby Hondo river.

Stores and saloons were already opening up as Crockett angled across the street to the livery and entered, finding his way to the stall in which the gelding was haltered.

Bellenger called from his office if Crockett needed help but Phil shook his head. The

44

gelding had already filled up with hay from the manger and after saddling and bridling the animal, Crockett watered it at the trough in the yard. He filled a canteen from the pump and slung it across the horn, afterwards inspecting the carbine in the saddle scabbard and also looking to the six-gun in his cartridge belt.

He bent down to adjust the latigo and tighten the cinch strap and heard the faint whisper of slippered feet coming from behind.

He turned and saw Maria in the entrance way limned by the brightening sunshine outside. He grinned at her and straightened up, leading the gelding by the reins to the open door.

'Buenos dias, Maria,' he said softly. 'I am riding, as you see; I guess I won't be back until tomorrow.'

She regarded him gravely for a moment, saying nothing, as though speech and questions were unnecessary. Then: 'You are going to the Eagle Tails, señor, to trail thees Vicente and hees gang? You mus' tak' great care. Vicente Tularez allows no one to come close to hees camp!'

'What do you know about Vicente?' Crockett asked the question idly, yet with a gathering suspicion darkening his thoughts.

Maria shrugged. 'Only what we all know, or rather guess,' she replied. 'No one 'as seen 'eem, not 'ees face. One two men 'ave gone to the Eagle Tails from time to time seeking Vicente's hide-out. But they 'ave not returned. That ees why I say be careful!'

Crockett nodded uncertainly, his thoughts still floundering in their sea of suspicion. He caught up the gelding's reins as a shadow fell across the threshold, and a fair-haired girl appeared. She said 'Good Morning' to Maria and then hauled up abruptly a few feet from Crockett.

'Thees ees Pete Crockett, Lucy,' Maria said. 'Señor Crockett – Señorita Lucy Shalless, 'Ondo Bend's school-teacher–'

'–and daughter of Seward Shalless, Hondo Bend's preacher,' Lucy finished, smilingly. She extended her hand and Crockett took it, gazing at her now and wondering how such a beautiful Northern girl as this one was came to be teaching Americano and greaser kids in such a place as Hondo Bend.

She had the bluest eyes imaginable and a creamy complexion which, so far, seemed not to have become impaired by the burning sun. Her hair was a coppery gold and cascaded in ringlets to the shoulders of her riding shirt. Around her slim hips she wore an ordinary whipcord skirt, which fell to the tops of small, spurred boots. As the skirt was not of the usual divided pattern, Crockett concluded that Miss Lucy Shalless favoured a side saddle.

'Glad to know you, Miss Shalless,' he said, recollecting himself and added, 'if you're heading out across the river, maybe I could ride along with you, a way?'

She shook her head, still smiling. 'Thanks all the same, Mr. Crockett, but I'm travelling south to a Mex village this side of Cactus Flats. Dad wants me to try to "convert" some of the Mexicans and also persuade them to send their kids to our school. There are not many schools in the southern part of Maricopa, as you may guess–'

'The school ees beeg enough to hold sixty cheeldren, señor, but Lucy 'as only feefeteen at the moment.'

'I see,' Crockett smiled. 'Well, I wish you luck, Miss Shalless. Sorry you're not riding my way.'

He touched his hat to both the women and swung into leather with the ease and familiarity of the veteran trooper.

He lifted the reins and murmured 'Adios,' turning the gelding onto the street and neck-reining it towards the Hondo, a quarter-mile distant.

In a few moments the scattered shacks and 'dobe buildings of Hondo Bend were left behind. Ahead wound the fringe of grey-green vegetation, brush and cottonwoods and willows which marked the banks of the Hondo in its dog-leg course towards the main Gila.

Crockett put the gelding to the river, whose level was lowering daily now. He went cautiously for fear of sand bars, but the animal found a firm gravel-bottomed footing and mid-stream swam the necessary few feet before its hooves struck the shingle along the opposite grade.

North of the river, Crockett paused long enough to shake the water from his boots and then produce the army field glasses which were carefully stowed at the bottom of his saddlebags.

He gave the hostile, arid country ahead his long, measuring glance through the glasses. Clumps of ocatillo, cat-claw, prickly pear, broke up the savage monotony of yellow rock and alkali dust. Here and there a vivid speck of colour betrayed the presence of a cactus plant in flower; occasionally a giant saguaro thrust upwards from the flat, dry country, offering its meagre patch of shade to the chance traveller. Far ahead, rising abruptly from the plains, the Eagle Tail mountains were a blue-grey lifting mass of jagged peaks and softly-shaded buttes, which marched down to talus slopes broken up by huge boulder and rock formations. Through the glasses Crockett could see the stark rocky canyons, twisting and winding their way across and through dried-up river beds and rock-strewn trails. It was broken country with a vengeance, savage and stark and barren and a man would have to know his way to the creeks and springs or else have the devil's own luck if he were to traverse that region and return safely and without mishap.

CHAPTER 4

ACTION AT MESA ROCK

Crockett had no particular plan in mind, other than to follow his nose and instincts. There was not the smallest chance of picking up any of Vicente's tracks which would long ago have been erased and filled by the steadily blowing dust.

Maria had said that Web Skogee and Frank Peck had travelled this way and once or twice, reminded of this, Phil thought he caught the faintest glimpses of partially covered tracks. Coming to a wide sweep of brown, sun-cured grama grass, he almost certainly identified two sets of tracks probably several days old. These were the tracks of the lawmen's horses and Phil reined in to rest the gelding, wondering whether the sheriff and his deputy had indeed conscientiously tried to trail Vicente, or whether the whole episode of that day's riding had been their way of throwing dust into the eyes of Hondo Bend's citizens.

The sun climbed higher in a brassy sky and more than once Crockett felt the ache of healing tissues in his back and along the backs of his thighs. Sweat stained the calico shirt and pasted it to his muscular body and sweat seeped from underneath his hat brim, running into his eyes and channelling a course through the alkali dust on his sunburned face.

He pushed steadily on at a slow, cavalry pace, conserving the gelding's strength as much as possible in this furnace-like land.

An hour after noon he found the thinnest trickle of water, winding through a patch of prickly pear and scrub. It was sufficiently deep, at least, to allow the gelding to drink and so save the precious water in the canteen; Crockett contenting himself with little more than a mouth wash from the lukewarm water in the bottle.

The afternoon sun blazed down and seared horse and rider with its burning touch, and Crockett, in between cursing the heat, wondered whether he were close enough in to the mountains for any of Vicente's men to be able to spot him crossing the wide expanse of scrub-dotted alkali and low bluffs.

Yet in spite of blistering heat and, at times, a scant four miles an hour, Crockett moved steadily nearer his goal, though by late afternoon, the lifting peaks of the main range seemed little nearer than they had done in the forenoon. It was then that Phil began turning in the saddle, looking backwards over the dry country, intuitively feeling that somewhere behind him, perhaps even far enough away to be completely out of sight, was another horseman, keeping his distance, yet following doggedly in the cavalry lieutenant's tracks.

Heat devils danced and shivered in the exploding heat of the afternoon and once or twice a water mirage appeared before Crockett's slitted eyes, but apart from the distant movement of some small animal seeking cover, there appeared to be no sign of human life anywhere across this parched expanse.

Crockett rode on, with an uncomfortable feeling that unseen eyes were watching him. He was more than ever convinced that somewhere along his back trail was some-one who knew all the answers to tracking a man, without himself coming into view.

Though his senses were ever alert, Crockett deliberately shut his mind to the problem of what lay behind him, concentrating now on the more important aspect of what lay in front of him.

He searched the recesses of him mind for stray bits of knowledge he had acquired about the Eagle Tails and the country ahead, and found that the sum total of his knowledge was small enough.

Some of the scouts at Fort Yuma had had occasion in the past to explore this broken country and in past conversation had passed on scraps of information to the lieutenant commanding C Troop.

There were innumerable canyons and rocky gulches, Crockett knew, in which a small army of men could hide; ideal places for an ambush where one man could snipe away at a large-sized posse just so long as his ammunition and water held out. Moreover, there were many plateaux and timbered benches stepped out along the mountain sides, ideal camping and hiding places, the scouts said, for roving Apache war parties as well as bandits and outlaws.

But for all the possible danger ahead, Crockett knew that the only way to play this was to make his scout and find out as much as possible the exact nature of the country and perhaps even pin-point, through his glasses, a few likely hide-out spots and landmarks which would serve him well, later on.

He remembered that the scout Bill Douro had, more than once, mentioned a place called Mesa Rock – a big, upthrust mass of colour-slashed rock whose flat top was thick with pine stands and brush vegetation. Here was such a place, Crockett thought, where one man could easily hold an army at bay, shooting down on them whilst remaining protected himself by the thick vegetation and timber of the table top.

Once again he drew the gelding to a halt and put his glasses to the foothills and the timbered slopes which shouldered upwards to the lonely white-tipped peaks. There was Mesa Rock! A beckoning sentinel to encourage – or lure – the lone traveller onwards! He could see the varying colours of rock strata, green, yellow, brown, white, as though the mesa had been cut with a giant knife. Crockett's eyes narrowed slightly as they glimpsed the faintest of ribbon-like trails curving round the base of the mesa. It looked as though that might be the way into the mountains, yet if that were so, and Vicente's gang were camped some way beyond, that narrow trail circum-navigating the rock would be covered day and night by at least one rifleman!

Crockett returned the glasses to his saddlebags and, with a quick glance at the westerning sun, began looking around him for a likely place to make camp. A brighter patch of green in the surrounding dun and grey-green terrain, caught his eye as he spurred the tired gelding forward.

By the time Crockett had reached the juniper stand, the sun was falling behind the hills to the south-west of the Eagle Tails, and, as he had hopefully anticipated, a thin, shallow creek meandered down from the foothills to lose itself somewhere to the west.

Within the thin belt of trees, Crockett found sufficient dry brush and deadwood to kindle a fire. He hesitated before lighting it and then, finally, with a resigned shrug, held the sulphur match to the brush. Whilst the piled up greasewood and mesquite kindled and caught light, he unsaddled the sweat-covered gelding and staked it out, feeding a little of the grain he had brought along with his own saddle provisions.

By dark he was hunkered down by the glowing fire, the smell of sizzling bacon assailing his nostrils and the aromatic scent of coffee drifting across the camp-fire on the warm evening breeze…

When Phil Crockett had ridden out of town, Maria Cordoba, with a murmured adios to Lucy Shalless, had recrossed the dusty main street to El Cuchillo.

Once inside her private parlour, she had immediately summoned Esteban.

The little wizened mozo had appeared almost instantly and with the privilege of a long-trusted retainer, had seated himself and had laid his bright, expectant glance on Maria's face.

'Señor Crockett has taken a pasear to the Eagle Tails,' she told Esteban in Spanish. 'It is a dangerous thing to do, travelling alone into the stronghold of Vicente's bandidos.'

Esteban nodded. 'It is like committing the

suicide,' he replied soberly, 'but perhaps you would have me follow the señor and see that no harm befalls him?'

'It has never been satisfactorily settled,' Maria said with apparent inconsequence, 'which are the better trackers, the Mexicans or the Apaches. An Indian, he will say the Apaches, of course. You, Esteban, would say any good vaquero could take up where an Apache finished, particularly when it comes to trailing *other* Mexicans!'

Esteban nodded again, accepting the praise with an objective-minded seriousness. 'It is, as you say, Señorita Maria; that is why I ask if you want me to follow the Americano?'

Maria smiled. 'Do not forget that Esteban is a tracker as good as any and that he has taught me all he knows.'

The Mex raised his brows. 'You go yourself? Alone?'

Maria nodded and Esteban came to his feet, knowing better than to argue with Maria de Mendoza y Cordoba and realizing at the same time that the girl was as capable as he at performing such a formidable-seeming task.

'I will personally see that a good horse is saddled and provisions prepared for you, Señorita,' Esteban said. 'What weapons will you take?'

'A knife, of course,' Maria said, 'and the

56

Sharp's rifle, with ammunition for it!'

She had left town by way of the tumble-down shacks and vacant lots behind Main, not wishing, for some reason unknown even to herself, to advertise her intentions or directions. Perhaps at the back of her mind was the thought that Señor Crockett himself would be annoyed if he discovered the girl following him and still more annoyed if she had made it known to the town.

All day Maria kept the man in front just out of sight. She had little difficulty in following the fresh tracks of Crockett's gelding; but apart from that there was little doubt in Maria's mind but that the Eagle Tails were his destination. She had told him as much in the livery, that morning, and although he had neither denied nor confirmed this, Maria Cordoba was quite sure in her own mind; sure enough at times to take little-known cut-offs so that she could sometimes ride parallel with Crockett, negotiating brush-choked barrancas and thus keeping out of sight should Crockett consider, as he obviously would, surveying his back-trail from time to time.

By the end of the day, Maria betrayed little outward sign that she had ridden nearly twelve hours in the desert's heat, constantly on the alert, not only for the man ahead but for possible enemies. At dusk, she dismounted and off-saddled the buckskin, hobbling the animal in approved vaquero fashion. She had gauged position and time well and in a little while she glimpsed the tiny winking light through the juniper stand which indicated that Phil Crockett had made his solitary camp.

Maria, dressed in black shirt waist and long black skirt contented herself with a dry camp, munching some of the cold tortillas and frijoles, which Esteba had packed in the saddle-bags. She had no worry over water, as the little Mex had provided her with two freshly filled canteens, one on the saddle-horn, the other, as a reserve, rolled in the serape lashed to the saddle's cantle.

Over her cold meal, Maria watched from time to time the small glow from Crockett's fire. She sat with her back against a low out-crop of rock, the serape around her shoulders, uncertain whether perhaps the man would move on during the night or wait until dawn before entering the foothills.

To this end, Maria stayed awake, catching herself nodding once or twice and reviling herself in soft, liquid Spanish for being so weak. She considered the vigil an absolutely necessary thing, if she were going to 'ride herd' on Crockett, as the Americanos would say, and be ready to help him if and when the time came.

Maria Cordoba was not unfamiliar with some of the narrow trails and paths leading upwards to the pine-clad slopes of the Eagle Tails. More than once, she and Esteban had travelled some way into the rimrock fastness of the lower foothills. But Maria had reason to believe that the crazy soldado from Fort Yuma was scouting the terrain for the first time and that he knew little enough of the possible dangers which lay ahead.

Thus Maria watched through the night, keeping her tired gaze on that ever-decreasing pin-point of light. An hour before dawn a cool wind rippled the warm breast of the desert flats and Maria hugged the serape closer about her shoulders and suddenly – fell asleep!

Maria awoke with a start, an odd feeling of imminent danger quickly bringing her to her feet. Even as she cursed herself for falling asleep during the time the sun had risen and had tipped the mountains to the east, she heard a distant shot, knowing at once that this was at least the second one. It had been an earlier rifle-shot which had awakened her.

With amazing speed now, she flung blanket and Mex rig across the buckskin's back, lashing the serape in place behind the saddle and swinging into leather even as she urged the refreshed and spirited animal forward at a dead gallop.

Horse and rider emerged from the small

bluff shelter of the overnight camp and hit the desert flats, veering round the juniper stand and making straight for the trail, clearly visible ahead as it wound around the base of Mesa Rock.

Maria touched spurs to the buckskin's flanks and the animal responded with a tremendous surge of power. Its long legs were bunched and outflung, as it tore off the miles and visibly reduced the distance to the rock sentinel at the base of the Eagle Tails.

Maria Cordoba, in spite of the long black skirt, sat the buckskin astride in the manner of the vaquero, the born horsewoman. She held the reins lightly and leaned her body forward in the stirrups to adjust her weight to the maximum benefit of the racing horse.

Under this killing pace, the Mesa Rock and the lifting mountains beyond, came rapidly into focus. But not fast enough for the girl who bitterly reviled herself for falling asleep at the worst possible time.

Once, her right hand swung down to the Sharp's rifle in its scabbard. She eased the butt and let the rifle fall back again. If she could but get into a position where she could use the damaging, long-range rifle, she might yet save the Señor Crockett from death and justify the course she had adopted.

The buckskin held gamely to the demanding pace set by its mistress and managed to reach the base of Mesa Rock before its breathing became too painfully laboured. Maria swung from leather, snatching the heavy Sharp's with her strong right hand.

She trailed the buckskin's reins and moved forward up the narrow, steeply ascending path, a black-clad figure of purpose, with an odd mixture of fear and resolve in her heart. She climbed higher, rapidly, seeming not to feel the sun's increasing heat nor the roughness of the rocky trail and with startling suddenness reached a point from which she could look down and observe the scene a quarter-mile or so ahead. And what she saw in that brief second survey, caused her heart to sink momentarily.

Crockett was astride his gelding but he appeared to be swaying in the saddle. His chin was dropped down onto his chest and what looked like a Winchester carbine lay amongst the stones and rocks nearby.

Two Mex bandidos were running now towards the wounded man; their horses Maria could glimpse tethered farther away at a clump of brush.

Both Mexicans were armed to the teeth; crossed bandaleros, knives and pistols and some kind of breech-action carbine was clutched by each of them.

The foremost was a scant twenty yards away from the barely conscious Crockett when Maria lifted the long black gun, resting it on the rock in front of her and running her eye along the dully gleaming barrel.

The narrow confines of the canyon were suddenly shattered by the explosion of the deadly Sharp's buffalo gun. Echoes reverberating around the high, rocky walls in ever diminishing volume. Blue-grey powder-smoke drifted from the rifle's muzzle across Maria's face and then she saw the sprawled figure of the nearest outlaw. His body twitched once and then was still. There was that grotesque twist to his limbs which almost certainly meant he was dead.

The second bandido had halted abruptly, fifty yards away. For a split second he raised his carbine to the barely visible black-clad figure behind the rock over a quarter-mile away.

He could see little of the sharpshooter and knew the futility of trying to dislodge such an accurate rifleman from such a strategic position. Furthermore, Juan Ramon Estenada had already glimpsed the completely unrecognizable face of his compadre, the heavy Sharp's slug having smashed the face and half the head away. Juan Ramon Estenada felt a little sick, but another roar from the Sharp's and a vicious geyser of dust at his feet induced him to forget his rolling stomach in the interests of safety. Immediate flight was the order of the day and Juan Ramon Estenada saw to it that his own orders were carried out adequately and comprehensively by his own willing body.

He zig-zagged along the path, flinging a backward glance over his shoulder every so often and then darting forward with lizard-like agility as more bullets spurted in the dust and ricocheted from the rocky walls on either side.

Whether the partly hidden gunman was trying to kill him or was merely sending him quickly on his way, Estenada had no idea. He prayed to the Holy Mother and his own particular saint, that the latter was the case and thankfully reached the tethered horses, putting himself round the bend in the trail in a half-fainting condition of sick fear and abject gratitude.

He was in the saddle long before he had recovered from his harrowing and frightful experience, quirting the horse unmercifully and brutally rowelling it with the wicked Mex spurs in his eagerness to be gone.

Maria smiled grimly to herself and then, in all humiliation, offered up a quick, silent prayer to the Madre de Dios.

A quick glance towards Crockett showed Maria he was still slumped in the saddle. Evidently he was not completely uncon-scious she thought and quickly retraced her steps down the trail until she came to the ground-hitched buckskin. She sheathed the rifle and swung aboard, putting the tired animal to the steep incline until they had breasted the top and had descended down through the narrowing walls of the canyon where Crockett's gelding still stood with wonderful stillness.

In a few moments Maria, with an amazing burst of strength, had half-dragged, half-lifted Crockett from the saddle. His tightly closed lids drew apart for a moment as he contrived to support his own weight, the better to help the girl. He gave her the briefest of smiles and put a hand to his thick hair, drawing the fingers away quickly and examining the sticky, red substance which now covered them.

'Lie over een that patch of shade, señor,' Maria said softly, half-supporting the wounded man with a supple arm around his waist. Together they managed it and with Crockett stretched out as comfortably as possible, his head pillowed on Maria's serape, the girl returned from the buckskin with a canteen and a jug of tequila.

She bathed the wound and ripped off a part of her left sleeve to form a wad. This she bound in place with Crockett's own yellow neckerchief.

His grateful eyes were on her now, as she sat back on her heels, surveying her first-aid efforts with a critical eye before putting the wine bottle to his dry, dust-caked lips. He drank long and appreciatively and managed a wry grin.

'This is getting monotonous, Maria, your rendering first-aid like this; the second time in our short acquaintance you've nursed me and doctored my wounds. Fortunately this isn't bad. I guess I was plumb lucky just to be creased. Lucky, too, that you were in the background with that long gun.'

'You knew what went on?'

'Only in a hazy kind of way,' he smiled. 'I heard another rifle – sounded like a heavy calibre Sharp's – and saw the first Mex hit the dust, but I was too goddam dazed to do anything about it. They could have taken me easy, if you hadn't been around. Say!' he muttered, turning squarely towards her. 'How come you *were* around in such a right timely manner?' Suspicion again darkened his thoughts and swam muddily in his eyes.

Maria regarded him with her level, sober gaze.

'You do not trust me, Señor Crockett, even after I 'elp you once, twice?'

He protested his innocence of such base thoughts and ingratitude, but the girl smiled wistfully.

'You try to feegure what I am doing here, pairhaps near Vicente's camp. How eet was I could be – Johnnee on the spot!'

He tried again to tell her that she was wrong; how deeply grateful he was, cursing himself at the same time for having such an evilly suspicious mind.

But she smiled again and laid a soft finger on his lips. 'Do not talk, señor. We 'ave to start back pronto. Othairs might've heard those shots. We do not know 'ow near or 'ow far ees Vicente's camp. Weel you try to mount, Señor Pheel – er – Pete?'

CHAPTER 5

DEPUTY WEB SKOGEE

'Sure I can ride, Maria,' Crockett grinned, 'and I guess we'd better get the hell out of here and fast. But I'm hankering to take a look at that dead Mex yonder.'

'I weel go for you,' Maria said quickly.

Again Crockett gave her his bright, appraising glance. 'We will both go, Maria,' was all he said.

They gazed down at the sprawled bandido who did not look so tough or brave, in death. Half his face had been blown away by the heavy Sharp's slug. Already flies and insects were crawling over the congealing mass of blood and smashed bone.

Crockett threw the girl a quick glance, which she intercepted. 'I have seen worse than that, señor. Do not worry, I weel not faint.'

Admiration stirred in him again, dissipating, for a little while at least, the recurring suspicions.

'I owe you a great deal, Maria,' he said almost inconsequentially and bent down to make his brief examination of the gruesome object. Above, black specks were wheeling about in the brassy sky. As soon as the humans had departed, the desert buzzards would swoop to their obscene task before a coyote or hungry cougar should scent the corpse.

Crockett was fishing in the thigh pockets of the dead Mex's skin-tight pants and already he had withdrawn a sizeable quantity of bills, silver dollars and gold eagles. He studied the money carefully for a while, Maria watching him intently with her deep, violet blue eyes.

Shortly, Crockett's glance lifted to the girl's face. 'This money,' he said. 'I'm almost certain it is part of the payroll stolen by Vicente's gang when they held up Fort Yuma's pay wagon and escort, just beyond Hondo Bend.'

'But you said–'

Crockett nodded and stood up, swaying a little with the effort.

'I know I did, Maria. I said I was after a deserter from Fort Yuma. Come, I will tell you the whole story on the way back. Let's go!'

As they rode, Phil Crockett, on this sudden hunch of his, told Maria everything; the true story; how the paymaster's wagon had been attacked and how the small escort had been caught one-footed, including the fact that Lieutenant Cass Cherry had been killed.

'It's not so much the dinero I'm concerned with,' Crockett said bitterly, 'though it's my main chore to recover it, or part of it, if possible–'

'You want to settle wit' the keelers of your amigo,' Maria said and Crockett nodded quickly.

'You've hit it, Maria, and thanks to you, one of the swine is dead already. Somehow or another, I've got to get Vicente's band out into the open, where they can be hit and hit hard.'

He kept twisting round in his saddle to study their back-trail, but there was no sign of moving dust from the now distant foothills at their rear.

'You haven't told me yet, how it was you were Johnny-on-the-spot,' Crockett said presently after one of his periodic surveys of the desert country in back of them. 'I guess perhaps you were the "hombre" I had a feeling was following me. If so, you sure did a good job of trailing.'

Maria smiled. 'Esteban has, over the years, taught me plenty. You weel know, of course, that the Mejicanos are amongst the finest trackers in the world. When you left town yesterday, I was ver' worried. I knew you deed not – realize exactly 'ow dangerous your scout was going to be–'

'So you followed on behind, armed with a Sharp's, water, tequila and a dam' fine buckskin?'

'You are not angree?'

Crockett laughed this time. 'Angry? How could I be when you saved my life? I guess you figure Americanos don't like being ridden herd on, by women,' Crockett drawled. 'Well, maybe they don't – generally. Me, I'm not so sure I don't like it!'

Maria flushed. 'You are not the hombre to 'ide behind a woman's skirts, nor was that my purpose. But sometime, a woman, she know a leetle better, pair'aps than the man?'

They made dry camp that night, near a shallow, dried-up river bed. The stars were bright in the velvet blackness of the desert sky. The cooking supper and coffee-pot wafted their savoury smells to the nostrils of the man and woman. There was a camaraderie here; the kind of camp-fire friendship and awareness that two saddle-partners find when hitting the lonely trails across a hostile land.

After supper, Maria leaned back against the saddle, a coffee cup in her hand, watching Crockett's lean, muscular fingers build a smoke. It was the girl who broke the long, pleasant silence as Crockett wiped a match alight and set fire to the quirly.

'We mus' decide on our story for town, Señor Pheel. You weel not want 'Ondo Bend to know you are after Vicente's band.'

'You're right, Maria,' Crockett said softly. 'Maybe Vicente has a "look-out" man in town. To let anyone know who I really am would be to tip off those greasers and maybe lose them altogether.'

He was silent a moment, thinking.

'Have you any good reason to have ridden so far from Hondo Bend, Maria? If so, it could be that I was just scouting the country, taking a pasear, and got myself shot down from ambush, maybe because the road-agent figured I was carrying a gold-poke or some heavy dinero.'

She nodded eagerly. 'There ees an old Mex sheep-herder, who leeves in a rancheria on the edge of the desert, mebbe seven-eight miles east from the juniper trees. I was visiting him and heard a shot. Pablo, that ees hees name, came up an' drove off the bandido. We brought you back to the rancheria and tended your wounds. We stayed the night in Pablo's hut. Tomorrow, I ride back weeth you to town. Ees that not good enough?'

Crockett nodded slowly. 'I guess it'll do, Maria, and no one can prove otherwise. What about Frank Peck, Web Skogee and the mayor? Do you figure any one of them might be in cahoots with Vicente's bunch?'

She remained silent a long moment, examining this question of his and mentally reviewing her total knowledge of these men.

'I theenk they are what they seem, Señor Pete. 'Olt Caddo, the alcalde, I am sure of.

The shereef, yes, I theenk so, and also Web Skogee, though there ees somet'ing about the dep'ty I do not like so much!'

Crockett lay back against his saddle, strangely and disturbingly content to be with this Spanish beauty. 'There's one thing, Maria,' he said at last, 'I reckon we'd both recognize the Mex who ran away. Even though I was muzzy, I remember he was a big fellow for a greaser and had a long white knife scar on his cheek.'

'Si!' Maria exclaimed. 'I remember too, now you say. Eet is somet'ing to go on, not much, but a leetle!'

Crockett stood up presently, spinning his cigarette into the glowing coals of the fire. He crossed over to the girl and almost roughly draped the serape over her shoulders and body. 'You sleep now, niña. I'll do guard duty tonight!'

Hondo Bend appeared to accept 'Pete' Crockett's story, particularly as it was more than corroborated by Maria Cordoba herself. Except that the lawmen and the alcalde were more demanding with regard to the details of the 'ambush.'

Crockett leaned against the bar in El Cuchillo, answering their questions slowly and feigning a dizziness from his head wound which he no longer felt, thanks to Maria's timely treatment.

Yes, he thought he might recognize the bandido again if he saw him, but Web Skogee and Frank Peck must know how difficult it was to be dead sure on such a matter.

No! There was no reason that he knew of, why he should have been picked as a likely gold-toting candidate. All Crockett wanted was to take a pasear round the country, perhaps even contact some of the outlying ranches.

'Well there ain't any spreads over to the Eagle Tails,' Web Skogee said curtly. 'You honin' to work, stranger, we kin put you in touch with Pothook or Three Feathers, the two biggest spreads around. Else you might find it healthier to travel on!'

Crockett regarded the deputy coldly, and like Maria felt there was something about the big man which savoured of the sinister. If the law, or any part of it in Hondo Bend, were crooked or in league with Tularez, then it would be the brick-faced Web Skogee on whom Crockett would make his bet.

He finished his drink now and spoke coolly, choosing to ignore the insinuations in Skogee's remark.

'I'll think on it, Skogee. The part about taking a riding job, I mean.' He gave the scattering of men at the bar a brief nod and walked slowly across the room and out onto the board-walk.

Across the street, Lucy Shalless was emerging from Bexar's Mercantile. Her glance came across and rested lightly on Crockett. She smiled as he crossed the dusty street with long measured strides.

'Buenos dias, Miss Shalless,' he said removing his hat. 'I hope you had some success at Cactus Flats. As I remember it you had a job of "converting" to do?'

She was not quite sure whether the tall stranger was laughing at her. For all her youth and lovely looks, Lucy Shalless was a girl who took life seriously, the more so since from early childhood she had been weaned on the zealous sustenance of her father's religion.

Now she rested the basket of provisions on the gallery rail in front of the mercantile and regarded Crockett with the sober speculation that a convert sometimes reserves for an unfortunate heathen.

'It is very difficult to draw these people away from their ancient beliefs and customs,' she said, answering his banter with full seriousness. 'But I *have* extracted a few promises regarding school attendances.'

'I'd sure attend classes myself,' Crockett drawled, 'if I could qualify on age.' He was surprised to see the colour wash into her fair cheeks and the sparkle in the blue eyes as she lifted her gaze to his smiling face.

'We have a class for older pupils,' she told

him. 'Father and I hold a mid-week service over at the tin chapel every Wednesday evening at eight. Also a morning and evening service on Sundays. We should welcome you to come – Mr. Crockett!'

C Troop's lieutenant, for once in his life, found difficulty in answering. He saw at once that she was in deadly earnest and that, for her, there was no question of joking about such a thing. Yet Crockett caught his first glimpse of the woman herself, beneath the outer cloak of the religion with which she covered herself. Her face was still flushed and her eyes retained that sparkle caused either by his own words, or because of the intensity of her feelings. Her lips were generously full, too much so to belong to an ascetic, he told himself, and her figure beneath the linsey-woolsey dress... He caught himself up suddenly and inwardly cursed as the soft colour deepened and stained her cheeks crimson. He had not realized how intently he had been regarding her.

'Let me carry your basket home for you.' Crockett hastened to make amends and was himself relieved to observe the change of expression in her eyes. She smiled now, and, womanlike, slid her glance back to his face from beneath half-lowered lids.

One moment the saint, the next the eternal coquette, he thought, but without censure of any kind in his mind.

He took the laden basket from where she was balancing it on the rail and moved along by her side as she turned upstreet, walking slowly past the stores and saloons and then angling across Main to a short side-street composed of a few 'dobe houses.

She led the way to a solitary cottage and Crockett, at her brief nod, pushed open the wicket gate.

'Perhaps you would care for a cup of coffee, Mr. Crockett?' she said, unlatching the screen door. 'I should like you to meet my father.'

It was too late now to draw back and with a murmured 'thanks,' he followed the girl into the neat parlour-kitchen.

Seward Shalless looked up from his chair at the table with a vague light in his blue eyes. He was a tall, spare man, that much Crockett could see even though the preacher was seated. He had long, flowing golden hair and beard, and his pale cheeks bore the bright hectic spots of colour which so often indicate the consumptive. He wore a white, starched collar, carelessly held in place with a string tie. His once black gaberdine frock coat was now dark green, rusty with age and weathered through exposure to the elements; it fitted his wide bony shoulders like a loose sack.

'This is Mr. Crockett, Father, who was

shot at over towards the Eagle Tails. Luckily he was only slightly wounded!'

'Ah,' Shalless exclaimed in a surprisingly thin voice. 'I remember your telling me this morning, Lucy. Neither men nor women are safe in this strange and wicked land, Mr. Crockett. Everywhere we see the hand of evil, the lust for gold as well as – er – other things.' He coughed slightly and gazed at Crockett blankly for a moment as though he had forgotten who he was.

Lucy was busying herself at the stove, pouring the hot coffee into cups and now bringing them to the table.

Seward Shalless reached for his cup with a long, bony hand, shovelling four-five spoonsful of sugar into his cup before half-apologetically pushing the sugar bowl across to Crockett.

Lucy opened her mouth to say something in a brave attempt to cover up her father's appalling manners. Crockett wished himself back in El Cuchillo yet, apart from common courtesy, which forbade any immediate exit on his part, he knew himself to be held there by the half-spiritual, half-physical beauty of the girl. If there was saintliness in her eyes, there was also a subtle invitation in her full-breasted figure...

Crockett cleared his throat, marshalling a polite phrase but was spared the necessity of immediate speech as boots pounded the gravel outside and Web Skogee entered through the unlatched screen door.

His smile of welcome for Lucy froze on his lips as he hauled up abruptly at sight of 'the drifting cow-poke.'

His black eyes darted rapidly from Crockett to the girl, as though demanding an explanation.

'Guess I didn't figger you had *visitors*, Lucy,' he sneered. 'Wouldn't have come bustin' in like that had I known–'

'You're always welcome, Web,' Lucy Shalless smiled. 'I guess you must know Mr. Crockett. Can I fix you a cup of coffee, Web?'

He nodded curtly, still addressing his remarks to the girl, though directing his bright gaze to Crockett's face.

'Figured Mr. Crockett had gone lookin' for a ridin' job,' he went on, speaking to Lucy's back. 'Said he was lookin' for work.'

'And I said I'd look in my own good time, Skogee,' Crockett drawled. 'Let *me* do the worrying about what I'm going to do! You tend to the job of rounding up bank robbers, or is that too tall an order for Hondo Bend's law department?'

Web Skogee's brick-red cheeks darkened still further, anger tightening his face and crawling up into his wickedly sparkling eyes. He came forward a couple of paces, his big fists tightening, as though here and now he would settle with this brash stranger, irrespective of the fact that they were both guests in the Shalless household.

Lucy whirled round from the stove, hurrying forward with the deputy's cup which she adroitly forced him to take, so negativing any possibility of rough action. Preacher Shalless continued to stare at the table, slowly stirring his coffee, alone in his own little world of strange hopes and dreams.

Crockett pushed away from the wall and placed his empty cup on the dresser.

'Thanks for the coffee, Miss Shalless,' he told Lucy. 'Sure hope your Mex niños turn up for school!'

He smiled at her and nodded briefly to Web Skogee who scowled back in return. Lucy held the door latch behind her back as Crockett stepped out onto the gravel path.

'Shall we see you at the service tonight, Mr. Crockett? Please come, if you can. Father is not always like he is today, but lately–' she broke off and bit her lips, her eyes glistening with unshed tears. She looked, Crockett thought, utterly beautiful; but what a hell of a life for a young and lovely girl!

'I can't promise,' he smiled, touching her arm lightly, 'I may be busy, it all depends. Meanwhile, adios, and thanks again.'

He turned his head once and saw her still

standing at the door, the sunshine painting her golden hair with a bright halation of light. Did she want another 'convert', or...? Crockett wondered about this as he lifted his hand in reply to her own rather pathetic wave...

Sheriff Frank Peck wiped his straggling moustaches with the back of his fleshy hand and shoved the empty shot-glass away from him.

He nodded briefly at Web Skogee who was still drinking Maria Cordoba's whisky.

'I'll be on my way then, Web,' Peck said. 'You keep an eye on things as usual?'

Web nodded, careful to mask the glitter in his eyes. This was what he wanted, for Peck to make his usual monthly ride to Sedge Jones' Pothook for an all night poker session. It was the sheriff's one weakness, this game at Pothook, and though he often sat in with Holt Caddo, Bexar and one-two others, several nights a week, the stakes here were small, not comparable to the exciting thrill of Sedge Jones' games. Moreover, last month, Frank had added considerably to his sheriff's pay by taking the pot. Tonight, therefore, Jones and the others would be all out to retrieve their lost money. It would make the game that much more exciting, and now Peck was anxious to be on his way.

No more anxious than Web Skogee was to

have him gone, for Web, choosing this night particularly, in view of the sheriff's being out of town, had an assignment himself. Vicente Tularez would be waiting for him at the rocks near Hondo Bend and like Peck, Skogee would be on the receiving end, only more so. Vicente was going to pay out far more dollars than ever Peck could win himself at poker; dinero which the deputy had coming *for his part in the hold-up at Hondo Bend.*

Without Skogee's valuable prior information, it was unlikely that even Tularez could have pulled off such a robbery. Now, Vicente, recognizing this in spite of his ruthless and grasping character, was ready to pay the deputy his cut and receive further information, if any, about the next army pay detail!

Out on the board-walk, Skogee watched the sheriff mount and point his horse along the south trail towards Sedge Jones' spread.

Skogee waited, a slow excitement stirring in him as he carefully smoked a cigar, nodding now and again to folk on the board-walk.

It was not only the prospect of meeting up with Vicente and receiving his sizeable share which caused the pulse to beat in Skogee's brick-red neck. He was also thinking back to the Shalless' cottage where, earlier in the day, he had seen Lucy again, even though the pleasure had been somewhat blunted by the presence of that damned Crockett bustard!

The preacher himself Skogee discounted completely. He grinned wolfishly in the night. Why, even if he kissed Lucy right there in the room, he doubted very much whether her crazy old coot of a father would notice, him being so far away with his thoughts of hell's fire and brimstone!

Skogee moistened his lips as he pictured Lucy at the stove, face flushed, full lips slightly parted, the curve of her body excitingly pronounced in close-fitting dress – en cuerpo, as the Mexes called it.

Skogee didn't kid himself that Lucy Shalless was not primarily interested in 'converts,' but she was a woman, wasn't she? And if Web's chances of having the golden-haired girl were better because of kneeling in the church and singing hymns twice a week, then, by hokey, he'd become as regular a church-goer as the most ardent catholic Mex!

These were pleasant thoughts for a man of Skogee's disposition and he stood there savouring them to the full, long after Peck had taken the trail to Pothook.

Presently, Skogee moved down the street towards his own shack, where, in the weed-strewn lot at the rear, he kept his own horse in a rude, makeshift lean-to. It was better this way, of course. He could come and go more or less as he pleased without the fool Bellenger or others in town knowing his movements.

He cinched the saddle onto the steel-dust, bridled the animal and led it out into the starry night. He made sure the carbine was in the boot and his six-gun in its holster, before climbing into leather and making his quiet and circuitous way towards the bend of the Hondo...

CHAPTER 6

SKOGEE TAKES A BEATING!

Once clear of the town, the deputy gigged the steel-dust forward more quickly in its curving course towards the out-crop of rocks which rose to form canyon-like sides where the river doubled back on itself. By the light from the sickle moon and stars, Skogee was quickly able to glimpse the spanish bayonet which grew in profusion at the entrance to a shallow cave, topped by over-hanging rock. This was the spot where the deputy always rendezvoused with the Mexican outlaw leader at certain pre-arranged times.

Not wishing to feel the sudden bite of cold steel or hot lead, Skogee sang out softly when he was some twenty-five yards away. He saw then the two shadowy figures moving in front of the small screened fire. Even at such a time as this, the deputy reflected, these dam' Mexes had to light a fire in order to concoct one or other of their filthy brews, else they were unable to go long without food and heated tortillas, frijoles or some of their evil-smelling fumado, careless of the possibility of discovery.

Vicente himself came forward as Skogee slid from leather and tied the reins to a low, stunted branch. Skogee grinned at the Mex outlaw in the moonlight. It always amused him that, despite Vicente's hard reputation, which included the killing of more than a dozen men, he always brought his lieutenant, Ramirez with him, explaining that it was necessary for his segundo also to take part in these discussions.

Vicente Tularez was a short, fat and greasy looking man with dark unshaven jowls, which wobbled, like his belly, every time he spoke. When he laughed, which was seldom, he gave the appearance of a vast and quivering jelly, but Skogee did not let the Mex know his thoughts, especially at such times as that.

'You got the dinero, Vicente?' Web asked as he joined them in the shallow cave near the low, but pungent-smelling fire.

'Si,' the outlaw assented. 'Ramirez 'as eet for you een zees sack. But mebbe you do not know; zere 'as been a leetle trouble?'

The deputy looked up enquiringly into the fat, oily face of this dirty but powerful little renegade who, on more than one occasion, had played both ends against the middle in Mexican politics.

Skogee shook his head. 'What kinda trouble, Vicente?'

Tularez said, spitting the words out with the venom of a snake, 'Thees goddam Americano, 'e weel haf to be rubbed out, sabe? 'E come to the Eagle Tail an' meet up wit' two of my men–'

Skogee's surprise was genuine enough. 'Say! That beats all hell! We heard back in town Crockett was takin' a pasear. He claimed some road-agent jumped him, thinkin' he was totin' a sizeable gold-poke, but he didn't say nothin' about two men or–'

Tularez waved a dirty, pudgy hand impatiently. He did not like being interrupted, least of all by gringo dogs.

'My bandidos would have cut him in leetle pieces,' the bandit snarled, 'but zere was another dog be'ind. When José heet thees gringo weeth hees first shot, 'e ran forward, but zees othair hombre, dressed in black, 'e shot from cover wit' a beeg gun an' Por Dios! José was no more! Juan, 'e come back queeck an' tell me what 'appened, but we were long ways from Mesa Rock where thees theeng she 'appen.'

'Mesa Rock, eh?' Skogee said thoughtfully. 'Crockett didn't say anything about going as far as that; they was supposed to be near the Mex sheep-herder's rancheria. And say,' he went on quickly, 'the hombre dressed in black you figured was covering Crockett, couldn't a' been anyone else than

– hell! it sure was a woman! *Maria Cordoba!*'

'Sangre de Cristos!' Tularez blasphemed softly. 'I 'ave 'eerd of thees woman. She ees no gringo but she no lik' Mejicanos, goddam!'

The small, lean Ramirez, silent hitherto, spoke now in a surprisingly rich, baritone voice. 'Maria Cordoba! As you say, Vicente, she do not love our compatriots. She prefer the Americanos. Yet thees man we speak of; 'e ees dangerous, si? 'E smell a rat. I theenk Señor Skogee een all our interests should – feenish 'eem!'

Tularez nodded so that his fat jowls quivered and the cast shadow from the chihuahua hat ran up and down his moon face like a window blind being worked rapidly. Ramirez was one of the few men the outlaw leader would ever listen to or allow to interrupt him.

'All this puts a different kinda face on things,' Skogee growled. He didn't tell Vicente that it would be a vast pleasure to liquidate Crockett. He was too smart for that. Instead he said, 'You figure this hombre Crockett is likely getting nosey, it might not be too difficult to settle his hash. Of course, I'd haveta cover up an' make the thing legal. Might even have to bribe a few witnesses. How dangerous do you rate a nosey "drifting cow-poke," Vicente?'

Tularez grinned and threw a wicked

87

glance at the deputy, afterwards rolling his eyes sideways to the smiling Ramirez.

'Eef thees 'ombre ees mebbe an ondercovair marshal, pairhaps, Señor Skogee, zen 'e ees likely to be dangerous to us bot', si?'

There was a long-running silence following the outlaw chief's words as Skogee digested the significance of Vicente's remark. What he had suggested, of course, was true enough, the deputy realized and felt a sudden thrust of apprehension as he considered the possibility that Crockett might indeed be an undercover lawman sent to probe into things at Hondo Bend and perhaps get a line on the Mex bandidos. In any case, it was now obvious that Crockett's story of an ambush by a road-agent was entirely false. He had ridden out towards the Eagle Tails deliberately, trying to get a line on Vicente's band. Somehow, Maria Cordoba had happened along or perhaps had ridden out with him in the first place. She, it must have been, dressed in her black shirt waist and riding skirt, who Juan had mistaken for another 'hombre.' The whole thing jelled, Skogee reflected. Moreover, everyone in Hondo Bend knew that Maria possessed a Sharp's rifle and furthermore, knew how to use it. Skogee himself had seen the Spanish girl blast a rock lizard into tiny pieces at a distance of over fifty yards when the small reptile had appeared no larger than a speck.

Skogee said now: 'Crockett may be no more than an interferin' drifter out for bounty money, Vicente, but either way I reckon you're right in sayin' he might be plumb dangerous. Leave him to me!'

Tularez nodded and gave his oily smile. 'You feex 'eem, Señor Skogee, lik' you say, but eef thees Crockett ride to the mountains again – pfft! *We* feenish 'eem off next time – no meestake, goddam!'

'Bueno!' Tularez continued, having finished with the problem of Crockett. 'What news of anot'er pay-wagon to thee Americano Fort?'

Web Skogee rolled and lit a cigarette and moved a little closer to the now dying fire. He talked quietly for a few minutes, whilst Vicente and his lieutenant listened in an eager silence...

It was still barely nine o'clock when Web Skogee clambered aboard the steel-dust and headed back to town, the dinero which he had received from Ramirez tucked safely away in his saddle-bags.

He returned by the same circuitous route which he had used to make his rendezvous with Vicente, and very soon approached his own shack from the rear.

Making quite certain that he was alone and unobserved, Hondo Bend's deputy crossed the weed-strewn lot, dismounting and off-saddling at the doorway of the small stable.

He removed blanket, saddle-bags and bridle, giving the steel-dust a good, quick, rub-down with clean straw, and forking a little hay into the tiny manger.

The saddle-bags across his arm, he moved to the rear door of his one-roomed shack and before lighting the single coal-oil lamp, carefully adjusted the gunny sack curtains across the windows. In a matter of minutes, he had pulled the blanket-covered cot away from the wall and had prised up a couple of boards in the roughly planked floor.

He reached down in the cavity and withdrew a fair-sized box which he opened by means of a key on his watch-chain. He riffled through the bills and coins which he had just received, making a rough check and with a satisfied grunt, deposited the money in the already well-filled box, locking it and returned it to its hiding-place.

Afterwards he replaced the floor-boards and shoved the cot back into its accustomed place.

He slung the now empty saddle-bags over the solitary hardwood chair and allowed himself a tight grin of satisfaction.

There were not many men, he thought, who would dare to play such a game, nor many who would care to work in with the notorious double-crossing, murdering renegade, Vicente Tularez. But Web Skogee knew, just so long as he was able to bring useful information to the Mex bandido, he, Skogee, was safe enough. Vicente, ruthless as he was, would be too smart to kill the goose that lays the golden eggs! Now Skogee fired a cigar, thinking his pleasant thoughts and planning what he would do with the future once he had amassed a considerable hoard. A man could do anything, he reflected, if he had sufficient dinero.

He turned the lamp low and stepped out onto the street from the front entrance of the shack, walking casually and unhurriedly towards Main and El Cuchillo. He went out of his way to greet one or two townsfolk, thereby establishing his own alibi, and remembered suddenly that this was the night he usually accompanied Lucy home from the weekly church service.

The clock in Maria Cordoba's place showed the time as a few minutes before ten. He still had time for a few drinks before he need walk down to the little tin chapel.

With three or four whiskies under his belt, Skogee began to feel even better than before. A pleasurable feeling of achievement and well-being rocked his senses gently as the whisky coursed through his body and set his brick-red cheeks tingling.

He nodded to Jeff for a last, quick drink, downed it and planked four silver dollars on the counter. He noticed that neither Maria, herself, nor the interfering bustard, Crockett, appeared to be around.

Thought of the blue-eyed, golden-haired Lucy sent anticipatory shivers across Skogee's back as he emerged from the cantiña and angled across the street towards the chapel, which stood alone at the end of Main under the shelter of an ancient cottonwood.

Skogee could see that most of the saddle-horses and buck-boards had gone. In a few minutes Lucy would emerge herself, perhaps questioning Skogee in that saintly but reprimanding way of hers, as to why he had not attended service tonight.

The deputy grinned in the darkness, wiping his mouth and moustaches with the back of his hand as he glimpsed the object of his thoughts coming out of the church and hesitating in the dark shadows of the cottonwood.

Skogee strode forward with all the arrogant confidence of a man who knew that he possessed a bold, physical attraction to most women. That those women were usually of a certain type, Web Skogee had never stopped to consider.

He came up to her now as she turned, hearing the sound of his boots as they hit the hard-packed cinders of the path with a solid impact.

'Why, Mr. Skogee!' Lucy exclaimed. 'So you *have* come to escort me home! I wonder you have the nerve after your absence from service tonight!' Her smile softened the reprimand in her words as Web caught her upper arms in his two huge hands. She saw that his face was more than usually flushed and a tiny, fluttering, half-fear, half-interest caused her breast to rise and fall more noticeably. Skogee's glance cut a swathe through the surrounding darkness. There was little light here save for that which still spilled from the open door of the chapel, and momentarily at least, the area seemed devoid of people.

Skogee's hands were still gripping Lucy's arms as he bent his head to her upturned face, using his weight and strength to press the girl hard against him. Even now Lucy Shalless was not quite certain of the deputy's intentions, but in a sudden stabbing and intuitive flash she wondered whether she might not have 'encouraged' him too much both with regard to these after-service walks and also the visits, innocent though they were, to the cottage.

For a moment then, her thoughts were cut off sharply as she felt his mouth hard and savage on her lips. She smelt the liquor and sensed more than understood, the primitive savagery of the man.

She was frightened for perhaps the first

time in her life; badly frightened and only then, through delayed reaction, started to claw and fight against his further advances.

Within the space of seconds, she realized she might as well be trying to ward off a mountain lion. The man had strength enough for ten such as she. Again his mouth found her lips as she fought desperately but with utter futility against his iron strength and wicked purpose.

She did manage to twist her bruised mouth away from his searching lips and in that brief moment of respite uttered a low, choking cry of despair.

Phil Crockett, smoking his after-supper cigar, and walking slowly towards the tin church for no other reason than a vague notion to see and talk with the girl, heard that low cry. He heard, too, Web Skogee's reaching laugh; it slammed against Crockett's eardrums so that its obscene quality seemed to ring on in his head.

Crockett saw them an instant after those telling sounds reached him, so that a quick anger stirred in him. Almost before he had dropped the smouldering cigar he was across the brown grass verge and over the cinder path, clawing at the man's silk backed vest so that it ripped from shoulder to waist in one complete tearing split.

Skogee whipped round, but thrown off balance with the quick action, found himself

94

unable to completely dodge Crockett's fast-travelling fist.

It hit him on the cheek-bone, bringing with it a slashing pain and the warm moistness of blood. From the corner of his eye, Crockett glimpsed the shadowed form of Lucy Shalless, as she stood with her back rammed hard against the cottonwood's trunk, her splayed fingers pressing into the bark.

Skogee had almost gone down with that first wicked blow of Crockett's but he recovered himself with surprising speed. His teeth were gleaming now in the darkness of his sweaty face as he came into the attack, enjoying a savage satisfaction as he felt and heard his hard blow thump into Crockett's body.

Phil staggered back slightly winded, realizing suddenly that Skogee was no push-over. He was a big, heavily muscled man and had had his share of rough-and-tumble fighting. He would bring his knee up or gouge out his opponent's eyes if the chance afforded and Phil adjusted himself to this quickly absorbed knowledge.

Crockett began parrying the blows, taking them mainly on his left arm, which was outflung and crooked to cover his upper body. He took one staggering swipe to the chin which rocked him back onto his boot-heels before he was able to regain the initiative and force the fight to Skogee's corner.

The deputy's face was glistening with sweat and blood, his barrel chest was heaving, yet he appeared well able to absorb the very maximum of punishment as Crockett came in again, using him now as a human punch-ball and delivering hard telling blows with all the strength at his command.

A misty curtain of red hate descended in front of Skogee's eyes as he strove desperately and bitterly to defend himself and return payment with interest. If he had disliked this Pete Crockett before, he now hated him with a deep and burning fury. Whatever the outcome of this fight, he would pay Crockett back, smash the man and make him suffer before finally snuffing out his light. He was no more merely a vague danger to the plans of Vicente and Skogee, he was something real and positive and hateful, to be dealt with as brutally as possible. Skogee would not want paying for the chore of rubbing out this bustard!

Such were the deputy's bright-flashing thoughts, even in the heat of the fight. Perhaps he knew now in a dazed, bleak way, that for the moment he was beaten. This drifting cowpoke had the strength and stamina of ten wildcats and even as Skogee lifted his hands to protect his bleeding and battered face, Crockett delivered the final smashing blow straight to the point of Skogee's jaw. Web swayed for a moment, spraddle-legged, his arms now down, his breathing tortured and his chest heaving, so that he emitted low rasping gasps. Then, strong as the man was, his legs buckled at the knees as he slowly crumpled and fell to the soft, churned up earth in the shadows of the cottonwood.

Crockett stood back, breathing deeply, wiping his wet face with the barcelona, the yellow kerchief at his neck.

Lucy came out of the trance-like fear which had held her through those brief moments of bitter fighting, in its rigid grip. Crockett turned and saw the pale blur of her face, the blue eyes now dark with the night's shadows.

'You've killed him!' Her voice was tight with horror, her whole body stiff and taut. Crockett smiled grimly and wiped the blood from his puffed lips. 'He'll be all right, Miss Shalless. Skogee's tougher than you think. He'll be out for a half-hour, maybe, no more. Come, let me see you home before there's any further trouble.'

Doubtfully, reluctantly, the girl allowed Phil to take her arm, gently shepherding her away from the scene and the still, sprawling figure of Hondo Bend's deputy sheriff.

CHAPTER 7

COURIER FROM FORT YUMA

This time, Crockett politely refused Lucy's invitation to 'come in for a cup of coffee.' For one thing he was not in the mood for being questioned by this girl, sincere as she was in her desire to 'convert'; secondly, he found her startling beauty strangely disturbing.

On the way back to the cottage he had answered her remarks and her thanks for his opportune intervention, with only a part of his mind on the conversation. Thus, he was relieved when she did not press the invitation further, but merely smiled and quietly closed the door on him.

Crockett turned and began retracing his steps towards Main and El Cuchillo, his thoughts now free to roam back over the incident of the fight and to speculate on the outcome. It was pretty obvious that Web Skogee would play the whole thing down, making some excuse for his battered condition without actually naming Crockett. It seemed to Phil that the deputy's mind would work that way. He would figure that just so long as Crockett made no mention of the fight or the reason for it, so long would Skogee himself refrain from telling the true story, knowing that not only Lucy Shalless would be involved but, more serious than that, trouble would surely arise if it were known that the lawman had molested Preacher Shalless' daughter.

Crockett was convinced that Skogee would play this close to his vest, even if it meant inventing some incident wherein the deputy had been beaten up by a bunch of unknown outlaws. Skogee would be smart enough to see that for Lucy's sake, Crockett would not give out what really happened and, as Crockett was scarcely marked beyond a faint bruise on the cheek and grazed knuckles, it was unlikely that anyone would notice sufficiently to point the finger at him as Skogee's assailant.

Phil thought that from now on the deputy would bear watching. How close he was to the sober truth of that, the lieutenant did not realize then.

He made for the patio entrance to the cantiña, intending to climb the back stairs straight to his room. He made the inside corridor without discovery, and then the kitchen door opened, flooding the gloomy corridor with bright light.

Maria emerged, holding the door half-open behind her, studying Phil's face with her serious and intent gaze.

Phil grinned and showed her his bloody knuckles. 'I was just going to have a wash-up–'

'Come eento the keetchen, Señor Pheel; there is no one there and I weel bathe that cut on your cheek before eet go all the colours of thee rainbow!'

He followed Maria into the kitchen where she set a bowl of warm water on the scrubbed table and brought clean cloths and medicaments.

He sat down in a rocker, feeling suddenly tired, his back aching abominably and his head throbbing from the bandido's bullet.

Maria gave him her long, measuring look and wordlessly moved to a cupboard, producing a jug of tequila, some of which she poured into a beer glass.

She passed the glass over and Crockett drank gustily until he had lowered the strong wine to within an inch of the bottom.

'Por Dios, Maria! I needed that. I–'

She smiled. 'Si. You 'ave been in a fight, that I can see and eet do your back no good and your head, she ees – muzzy!'

Phil laughed. 'Heck! You know too much about me, Maria. Mebbe you know I've just thrashed Skogee for – interfering with Lucy Shalless!'

She shook her raven black head, her eyes wider now. 'I deed not know, Pheel. But that ees bad. You mak' an enemy of thees Skogee. Do not forget 'e ees a lawman. He could shoot you down and claim you drew first.'

Crockett nodded, his face sobering as he studied the Spanish girl from under his drawn down lids. She was certainly smart. Weren't many women who would have thought of that point about a possible bushwhacking, so quickly.

He rolled a cigarette and smoked it quietly, while Maria bathed the cuts on face and knuckles, afterwards spreading a Mexican paste over the cheek wound which she assured Phil would take away any discolouration by morning.

Crockett was content to relax under the wonderfully gentle ministrations of this surprising girl. He began to compare relative looks and qualities and then quickly threw out the thoughts, disgusted at himself for weighing up Maria and Lucy in his mind as though they were prize heifers for the buying!

Shortly, Maria stood back and nodded. 'You weel look all right tomorrow, Señor Pheel – er – Pete! Bueno! Now I feex you some coffee, si?'

Crockett opened his eyes. The tequila made him feel damnably sleepy; that on top of the fight; but he also felt more relaxed now and, momentarily at least, contented.

He watched the girl in her tight-fitting black silk dress, en cuerpo, admiring the lissom, yet rounded, figure, the deft hands and shapely arms bared now to the elbows as she poured coffee from the pot into two cups.

She pushed one towards him and sat down opposite, stirring sugar into her own cup.

''Ow does eet go, Señor Pete, thees search for Vicente's band, and what deeference you figure thees fight with Skogee will mak'?'

Crockett gave her a brief word picture of his tangle with the deputy, confining himself to a terse report.

'I'm figuring Skogee won't talk much about this, except to concoct some story or another for the benefit of Peck and Caddo and the town in general.'

'And *you* weel say not'ing?'

He nodded. 'It's obvious of course that Skogee can't prefer a charge for assaulting a lawman without involving himself. As to his private and unofficial reactions, well, I figure like you do, Maria, that he'll bear watching and so will my back!'

She inclined her head in agreement. 'Already, once, you 'ave felt Skogee's shot-gun; thees time you mus' watch weeth eyes in the back of your head, for a carbeen or seex-gun!'

'The time has come, Maria,' Phil said, 'to

get a little action. I've been gone from the fort nearly a couple of weeks and all I've succeeded in doing is to get shot at with monotonous regularity, and if it were not for you, I guess I'd be in a dam' sight worse shape!'

She flushed, yet she did not drop her gaze. She said, 'Ees there any way I or Esteban can 'elp you, Señor Pete?'

He thought for a moment, his mind and his whole body now stimulated by the coffee, the attention to his wounds and everything about the woman sitting opposite him.

'There may be, Maria. Esteban particularly might help. Soon I shall be sending a message to Major Blaine Mitchell at Fort Yuma. I could go myself but I might lose an opportunity that way.'

'Esteban weel go for you, when you say the word,' Maria said simply. 'Now you should go to bed and rest.' She turned away as Crockett rose and crossed to the door.

'Buenos noches, Maria,' he murmured.

'Buenos noches, señor. Sleep well and pairhaps you weel dream of a fair-haired Americano weeth the so beeg blue eyes!'

This day seemed hotter than the preceding ones. Hondo Bend lazed in the oven-like temperature of afternoon and Crockett found the shadier parts of the walled patio, irritable with the aches in his body and impatient with himself in particular.

He knew that Blaine Mitchell must be wondering what things C Troop's lieutenant had discovered, if anything, and Crockett was forced to admit to himself that it was precious little. But in spite of that, it was very necessary to get in touch with Major Mitchell soon. Crockett wanted to know about the relief pay-detail which no doubt the army at Prescott would very soon be escorting as far as Phoenix. After that, the Fort Yuma detail, who would have ridden to Phoenix specially for the job, would take over, as they did last time.

But on this occasion, Crockett promised himself that Vicente would have a different kind of reception from the previous one. This time, the information would go out, as bait, that the paymaster's wagon was even more thinly escorted and that the strongbox carried next month's payroll as well.

For the third time Crockett tore up the piece of paper on his knee and ground it savagely under foot. It was all right for Esteban to ride to Fort Yuma with the message, but it was a hell of a thing to try to write down all the things that had to be said and the questions which Phil wanted to ask his commanding officer. It was not so simple as an ordinary field report on some decisive action. Here, everything was hypothetical and vague; there was little factual information. Maybe it would be better to ride back to the fort and see Mitch himself. But again Crockett shook his head impatiently at the idea. It would take at least three days each way and to be away from Hondo Bend for nearly a week might prove disastrous. Phil had the idea that here in Hondo Bend lay the key to the situation. It was a vague ephemeral feeling with no real shape or substance, yet he felt convinced that if he were away too long, something unpleasant, maybe tragic, would happen.

He leaned against the back of the bench, feeling the sun's heat strike and burn him, bringing the sweat to his face and neck and arms...

A short distance away on Main, a rider urged a weary, alkali-stained gelding towards the trough in front of the blacksmith's shop. The man was dressed in the uniform of the Federal Army and wore a sergeant's stripes on his blouse sleeves. He sat immobile as the gelding drank long and gustily, yet the man's blue eyes in the saddle-leather face took in more details of Hondo Bend in those few minutes than many a citizen had done in his whole lifetime.

Shortly, the sergeant pulled his reluctant mount away from the trough, now openly surveying the town as though giving it his first enquiring look.

A voice spoke from the shadowed gallery in front of the sheriff's office. 'You lookin' for a drink, soldier, try El Cuchillo, right over there!'

The sergeant turned and grinned. It was more as though his leathery face split in two. Sweat runnelled the dust on face and beard alike, but the heat seemed not to cause this raw-boned Irish sergeant undue discomfort.

'I'm thinkin' that's a right good idea, Sheriff,' Sergeant Bryne Ewart drawled. 'There's no business, even an army courier's, so urgent a man cain't wet his whistle.'

Frank Peck nodded. But for the fact that he had been cleared out by Jones and the other players at Pothook last night, he would have welcomed the chance to join this soldier from Fort Yuma at the bar of Maria Cordoba's place.

He watched while the cavalryman tied the gelding so that the animal's head caught the minute cast shadow which spilled from the walk-roof onto the hitch rack. Then Ewart tromped across the street and pushed through into the cool 'dobe interior of El Cuchillo.

This was the first time that the top sergeant of C Troop had been in here and a surprised pleasure showed itself on his lean, reckless face, the more so when Jeff produced a glass of ice-cold beer which Bryne downed in a single long gulp. He wiped mouth and moustaches and signalled for another one, his eye on the little wizened Mex who had suddenly darted from the room through a rear door. He wondered idly at this, as he drank his second beer more slowly, enjoying the coolness and the bite as it ran over his scarcely moistened tongue.

He saw the woman then and stopped drinking instantly, holding his glass poised in mid-air as he ran his frank and admiring glance over her. The Irishman who does not appreciate a beautiful woman is not born, neither will he ever be born to this earth and Sergeant Bryne Ewart was no exception. His blue eyes sparkled, and once again his black-bearded face split in a grin of pure enjoyment.

There were two ways a man could look at a woman and Maria had seen them both. This was the full-stare of sheer admiration and although bold enough to make a woman's colour mount, it brought a smile to Maria's lips and pleasure to her heart instead of anger or contempt.

Her lips still curved upwards as she came towards the solitary uniformed figure, giving the scattering of other drinkers the benefit of her welcoming glance.

'The saints be praised for ever directin' me

own footsteps to Hondo Bend and El Cuchillo,' Ewart grinned, placing his half-empty glass on the polished redwood. 'And if I never believed in angels on the earth before, then I'm sayin' it's a shocking disgrace I am to the regiment and the fort its own self!'

'Welcome to El Cuchillo,' Maria smiled. 'And would eet be Fort Yuma you speak of?'

Ewart nodded. 'None other,' he said, 'and I'm on me way to Phoenix, more's the pity, else I would be stayin' on here to spend the rest of me life–'

Maria cut him short with a sweep of her arm and a curving smile. 'You Ireesh troopers! You no fool Maria Cordoba!' She came closer now and, under cover of the general conversation, spoke softly.

'Would you by any chance be lookin' for Señor Pheel Crockett; pairhaps to geeve heem a message from the fort?'

Bryne Ewart's face grew wary. 'I might be, señorita, if you happened to know where he's at!'

'Feenish your drink, sergeant; the señor ees out back een the patio. I theenk 'e 'as been 'oping for news from your Encomendero!'

Ewart grabbed his glass and drained the contents quickly. 'Make it slow and easy, señorita, like you might be showing me where to wash up!'

She nodded. 'Follow me, sergeant,' she murmured, 'you can 'ave a meal 'ere too, eef you lik'.' She led him through to the rear of the house, along the corridor and out on to the patio.

Crockett was pacing up and down now, unmindful of the sun's heat, a worried frown on his face. He swung round as the sound of cavalry boots slammed hard against his ears. He took in the situation in a second and the frown was erased by a grin of welcome.

'You old sonofagun, Sergeant,' he growled, coming forward. 'Have you got news from the major?'

Sergeant Bryne Ewart was unable to suppress his grin of pleasure, but he jumped smartly to attention and saluted his senior lieutenant.

'Relax, Bryne,' Crockett said, never one to insist on observing the wide gap between officer and man. He glanced at Maria, who was turning away. 'Stay, Maria. You're in this now whether you like it or not and I guess it was you who found Sergeant Ewart and brought him to me?'

'Esteban in thee first place,' Maria smiled. 'Now let us seet in the shade, si?'

The three of them relaxed on the bench in the shaded alcove, all formality discarded while Crockett told his sergeant what had happened.

Then Ewart drew a large envelope from the inside of his tunic. 'With Major Mitchell's compliments, sir, and he said for me to help you in any way you want.'

Crockett nodded and tore open the envelope, reading through the foolscap sheet of information penned in Blaine Mitchell's own precise handwriting.

Phil looked up when he had finished reading and the others saw the gleam of purpose sparkle in his eyes.

'You know what's in here, Bryne?' Crockett asked, tapping the letter with his finger.

'Sure I do, sir. It was the major himself told me in case I could be of use to you.'

Phil turned to the dark girl, from whom Ewart found difficulty in keeping his eyes.

'This is detailed information of a plan I touched on with Major Mitchell before coming here,' he explained. 'The major's fixed for an army pay-wagon to leave Phoenix tomorrow, Friday. It will arrive in Hondo Bend probably on Saturday night. The escort detail will rest up and proceed on its journey to Fort Yuma on Sunday. But there will be a big difference,' Phil told them grimly, 'between *this* pay detail and the last one! Inside the canvas-topped wagon will be twenty armed troopers, but to all *outward* appearances, the pay-wagon will be only thinly escorted by five mounted troopers. In other words, Maria,' Phil smiled, 'there will be twenty-five well-armed fighting troopers to meet Vicente, this time!'

'How weel you let Vicente know about thees detail?' Maria said.

'I reckon he'll know all right, same as he did last time, but just to make certain the sergeant here will get slightly liquored up and start shooting off his mouth about the amount of dinero which is being sent this time to Fort Yuma. I'm still convinced that there's someone in Hondo Bend, either directly or indirectly connected with Tularez' gang and who tips him off with information!'

'Then, when Vicente attacks thee wagon, 'e weel be in for one ver' beeg surprise, huh?'

Phil nodded. 'I sure hope so. That mal hombre has one hell of a lot to answer for,' he growled. 'You, Bryne, can start in right away getting "liquored up," but not so much you get really drunk!'

Ewart grinned. 'Leave that to me, sir. If there *is* a rat in Hondo Bend who's in with this bandido, he'll soon know all about the pay-wagon and the amount of dinero it's carrying!'

'One more thing,' Crockett said. 'You'll see me around town and in El Cuchillo, but you don't *know* me, sabe?'

'And what would an army sergeant be

111

doin', drinkin' with a footloose saddlebum?' Ewart wanted to know, his blue eyes twinkling.

'You weel ride back weet' the detail on some excuse, Pheel?' Maria suggested.

Again Crockett's surprise was sharp and sudden at the way this woman put her finger on the pulse of every situation.

'Yes, Maria. Maybe I'll even give out I'm volunteering to join up. Anyway, I shall ride back with the escort which is even now on its way to take over at Phoenix. But they won't be riding through here on the outward journey!

'By the way, sergeant,' Phil said, tapping the pocket into which he had now thrust Blaine Mitchell's letter. 'The major doesn't say who is in charge of the detail?'

'Lieutenant Martin, sir, is in command, and all the men are from "C" company. They have all been briefed about this thing and will be waiting for you to give the word.'

Crockett nodded. 'I see. All right, Bryne, you get a few drinks down you and start the ball rolling about the pay detail coming through on its usual route on Saturday night. After that, you'd better climb into leather and be on your way to meet them.'

'That's right, sir,' Ewart said, coming to his feet and grinning down at Crockett and the girl. 'I'm supposed to be carrying letters to Phoenix. Reckon I'd best head out about dusk after I've spread the word.

'Just one thing, sir. Supposing Vicente doesn't bite?'

Phil shrugged. 'We don't lose anything even if he doesn't, but somehow I think he will if we make the bait tempting enough!'

CHAPTER 8

WEB SKOGEE SENDS WORD

Between late afternoon and dusk it seemed to Hondo Bend that the courier-sergeant from Fort Yuma had consumed just about as much liquor as he could hold. One or two townsfolk, such as Bexar of the mercantile and Jud Little, the saddler, voiced their disgust in no uncertain terms. Not that they cared a fig about a man drinking too much; it was just that *this* particular hombre was an army sergeant and, as Bexar growled, watching Ewart make three tries before reaching the McClellan saddle, 'To hell with an army man who gets drunk on duty and shoots off his mouth. Serve 'em dam' right if they lose *this* pay-roll. They're sure askin' for trouble.'

Jud Little nodded and spat disgustedly. 'Good thing he ain't escortin' civilians through the territory else they'd all end up minus their scalps, fer sure!'

'Or buzzard meat for Vicente's gang,' Bexar grunted, turning back to El Cuchillo.

Out on the dusk-shaded board-walk, Crockett leaned against the cantiña's front and grinned to himself.

He didn't blame men like Bexar or Little for their condemnation of the army, particularly as Sergeant Ewart had given an excellent performance. He had apparently consumed a prodigious quantity of both tequila and whisky bought by himself and also several beers to which one or two of the more liberally minded townsfolk had treated him in their astonishment and desire to see just how much this black, raw-boned Irishman *could* hold!

But if they had thought to witness him pass out and sleep it off for twelve-fourteen hours, they had been disappointed. Ewart's eyes were half closed and the leather cheeks where the moustache and beard did not cover them were dark and sweaty.

Even then, when he had pushed himself away from the bar, they were more than amazed to see that he still contrived to stand, spraddled-legged, swaying until he took a firmer grip on himself and weaved uncertainly towards the door.

He seemed to have some slight difficulty here, but it wasn't enough to stop or floor a fighting trooper! He made it all right, and the watchers in El Cuchillo tacitly moved to the doors, following his drunken progress across the board-walk towards the gelding at the rack.

Frank Peck and Holt Caddo watched in amusement and behind them, Web Skogee's dark eyes took in everything with more than average interest. During those couple of hours' solid drinking, Skogee's ears had been alert as well. Like the others in El Cuchillo he had heard plenty, but it was this man Skogee, this lawman, who was the one determined to use the knowledge gained for his own ends! He wouldn't be able to go to Vicente himself, but he would send a rider just as soon as he could reasonably get away from the sheriff!

For twenty dollars, Yuma Jack would ride to the Eagle Tails and contact Vicente. For twenty dollars, Skogee thought, with a grin, Yuma Jack would ride through the very fires of hell...

Phil Crockett's chair was tipped back against the wall. In the near full darkness beyond the reach of the cantiña's bright lit windows, he was a deeper shadow without shape or form. The tip of Crockett's cigar glowed evenly as he sat back to all appearances an idle and lazy drifter.

But from this particular spot in front of El Cuchillo, Crockett was able to keep his eyes on most of the main points in town. He could see the extreme corner of the livery; the two saloons and one cantiña further on; the first intersection, the right-hand street of which led to the Shalless cottage. By turning his head in the opposite direction, he could see where Mex labourers were still

116

working on the wrecked bank, making their casts of 'dobe brick overnight, and waiting patiently for them to bake hard in the next day's sun. They were being paid good wages plus bonuses for this work and it was all the same to them working in the light of naptha flares, as it was sweating during the day. No threats or bribes, however, would induce them to relinquish their three-hour siesta every afternoon and Crockett grinned at the thought as he watched the silhouetted figures pass slowly backwards and forwards beyond the ring of flares.

He went over in his mind the things that could or might happen during the next week. Nothing was certain, however, beyond the fact that Giff Martin, Phil's junior fellow officer, would bring the pay-wagon detail from Phoenix via Hondo Bend either Saturday night or Sunday morning; probably the former.

They would rest men and horses over-night in town and mount guard duty on the wagon as per instructions. For so short a time they would not place the army strong-box in the bank even supposing the bank had been rebuilt and refitted.

How Giff Martin would work it, so as to keep the twenty wagon troopers out of sight, whilst the detail was in Hondo Bend, Phil wasn't sure. But he guessed that Martin would have Sergeant Emery in charge of

117

them and would evolve some plan whereby the men would make a secret overnight camp and then join up with the wagon and five-trooper escort later, on the Sunday. Just so long as the twenty left the detail and returned to it without being spotted, things should go without a hitch. After Vicente had pounced, Crockett considered, would be time enough to decide whether their ruse had failed or succeeded. He hoped to God it would succeed, not so much on account of the money but because the murdering bandido or one of his men had killed Cass Cherry–

His thoughts were suddenly cut into as Frank Peck and Skogee emerged from the cantiña. Phil and Skogee had not come face to face since the fight and, presumably, Skogee had given some explanation of how he had received the damage to his face.

Crockett watched them now as Peck separated from his deputy and wheeled away towards the lamplit sheriff's office. Leisurely, Skogee rolled and lit a cigarette. It was obvious that he had not seen Crockett sitting there in the blue-black shadows of the gallery.

Shortly, he descended the walk, angling across the street and dodging between riders coming in and one-two ranch buckboards.

On a sudden hunch, Crockett arose,

grinding out the half-consumed cigar under his boot. He followed in Skogee's tracks, the darkness of the night, relieved only by splashes and pools of yellow thrown from saloon and store, sufficient to cover him from the deputy ahead, should he chance to look back.

But Skogee didn't appear to be worrying about the possibility of anyone following as he strode on, his long reaching strides soon bringing him to a narrow alley-like street, wherein were a few small 'dobe houses and one or two derelict looking shacks. It was towards one of the latter that Skogee moved and this time he did glance round, making sure that this part of town was momentarily free of people.

Crockett was still in the deep shadow of the corner building, and stood so still and quiet that Skogee wasted no more time in entering one of the tarpaper shacks.

Crockett considered the advisability of creeping right up to the shack in an attempt to see or identify the owner and perhaps overhear some of the conversation. It was not often, in a situation such as this, that caution laid its restraining touch on Phil Crockett's actions, but now it did. Almost it seemed against his better judgement he remained where he was in the shadow of the darkened store which had been shut up for the night.

There was the thin thread of an idea running through Phil Crockett's mind and it had to do with this Web Skogee. It was possible, he thought, and the more he examined the idea the more he was inclined to think there might be something in it. Skogee was in a position, as a lawman, to obtain information of almost every kind which would be useful knowledge to a bandit!

It was no longer an instinctive caution which caused Crockett to remain where he was, it was the wariness born of this sudden thought and the following line of reasoning. For, if Skogee were involved in anything with Vicente and his gang, then it was better to let the thing ride on to its ultimate climax which, Crockett figured, would be the raid on the paymaster's wagon!

If he were to interfere now, and run the risk of discovery, the plans that had been and were being made to lure Vicente into the trap, might well be ruined.

As it was, Skogee did not spend long in that dimly lit tarpaper shack. Crockett saw him reappear within ten minutes and stand quite still as though listening or thinking. For a moment Phil wondered whether Web had spotted him, but he quickly realized this was not the case as another man appeared round the side of the shack leading two saddled horses.

It looked as though Skogee had been scouting the street, for all he did was to wave the man on impatiently.

It was too dark in this deserted quarter for Crockett to be able to glimpse anything of the other man's features. He saw little enough of his shape as he swung up into the high Mex saddle of the nearer horse and hit leather with a surprisingly sharp slap that carried easily to the watching man's ears.

Phil caught the barest glimpse of a slim, slightly-built shape topped by a conical chihuahua hat. No Americano wore such headgear, therefore the man was a greaser, Crockett figured. Further evidence of this was contributed by the way the horse reared at the touch of the wicked Mex spurs. In a matter of seconds, the horseman was leaving town at a fast clip, taking along the spare saddler on a lead rein.

That meant, Crockett thought, he was going to make quite a journey. Further more, he was heading towards the Gila slightly more westward than north, which indicated, unless he were being foxy, in regard to his direction, he was heading plumb for the Eagle Tails!

Crockett did not disregard the possibility that the Mex might easily be heading for some village or small town, anywhere west or north, but it was a surer bet that the rider's destination was the far off Eagle Tails wherein Vicente Tularez had his hide-out, else why take two saddled horses?

Crockett delayed no longer. Already the Mex horseman was almost lost in the night shadows; any second now, Skogee would wheel round and start walking quickly back to Main or else his own house, wherever it was.

Crockett backed away, careful to move his feet in slow, long strides so that the spurs would not sound off their warning.

He breathed a sigh of relief as he gained Main Street and became just another figure in the noise and bustle of the evening's activities.

He was hungry now and could go a drink for that matter. The thought was warming as he moved unhurriedly now towards El Cuchillo. After he had eaten he would find Maria and tell her about Skogee and his suspicions of the man. For Maria Cordoba had bought herself into this game, Crockett thought, right from the time she and Esteban had dragged him in from under the boots of the law and had dressed his wounds. Again when she had followed him to the Eagle Tails and had beaten off the attack by the two bandidos, killing the one and sending the other running with Sharp's slugs to help him on his way!

It was strange that Crockett should have suddenly thought back on this incident again, at this precise moment and had speculated on the other bandido, remembering the knife scar which he had glimpsed that once before almost passing out from the bullet wound in his head. Strange in a way, because Crockett was to meet the bandido again, very soon and very suddenly!...

He pushed through the doors of this place, which in so short a time had become almost as familiar to him as his own quarters at the fort.

El Cuchillo was not crowded, this being the time when most folk were partaking of an evening supper. Afterwards, there would be drinks, games of chance, the usual things to while away an evening and a few hard-earned dollars.

Crockett leaned against the bar and grinned at Jeff. The two men had long since sized up the other and in each was more than a hint of respect for the other man. Phil Crockett had, over a period of nearly a week at the cantiña, weighed Jeff up as a hard, tough and capable hombre, who had no trouble in determining where his loyalty lay. Apparently, four-five years ago, when Maria and Esteban had first come to Hondo Bend, they had picked Jeff up out of the gutter, had sobered him up and had offered him the job as bartender. There would be no pay until they were on their feet but Jeff was broke and jobless anyway and particularly cagey about his past.

Maria had made her decision and, as is often the case, intuition had proved more conclusive than logic. Jeff had worked well, and his love and affection for the Spanish girl was of the dog-like variety. He would have cut off his arm to save her grief and Maria, quick to realize and appreciate the dumb devotion of this hard character, showed her gratitude in a practical way. That was how the 'commission' idea had been born.

For his part, Jeff knew enough now to understand that 'Pete' Crockett was, in all probability more than a drifting cow-poke. His first fears that Crockett was a marshal sent to investigate Jeff's own back trail in life, had been quickly dispelled by Esteban. Whatever Jeff knew as to what was going on, however, the three of them knew he could be trusted not to shoot off his mouth. As to Sergeant Bryne Ewart's deceptive play during the later afternoon, Jeff had been told that the army man was doing that under orders and for a specific purpose. Thus, much of the 'tequila' and 'whisky' had been little more than the coloured water the percentage girls usually drank.

'What'll it be, Pete?' Jeff asked, wiping the already shining top of the bar and reaching for a rye bottle with his left hand.

Crockett nodded and said, 'Pour two, Jeff.' He looked about the big room, identifying and acknowledging one or two of the towns-folk drinking at a card table. At the roulette layout, Gonzales the houseman, was idly spinning the wheel and flicking the ball, working on some 'infallible' system of his own.

'Have you seen Skogee's face?' Jeff asked, clinking his glass against Crockett's with a murmured a vuestra salud!

Phil's expression was one of bland inno-cence. 'Haven't seen Skogee since yesterday, at least, not in the light. What happened?'

Jeff gave the other man a slow, appraising stare. In back of the grey-green eyes was a hint of amused disbelief.

'Claims he got so plastered he didn't know which way he was comin' and landed full tilt into the back of a loaded spring-wagon out on Spanish Street. Said even that didn't sober him up properly and by the time he *did* manage to get up an' stagger home, his face was in a bad shape!'

'You don't believe the story, Jeff?'

The bartender's poker gaze was on the slightly grazed knuckles of Crockett's right hand as it rested on the counter. He lifted his eyes now to Phil's face. 'I cain't figure how he could've hit the spring-wagon with the *backs* of his hands,' Jeff said mildly, smiling a little now. 'Can you?'

Before Crockett could answer, two things happened simultaneously. Maria emerged from the dining-room, pushing the drapes aside as she came towards the bar and outside the sharp rataplan of hooves sounded hard and clear against the softer noises of the night.

There was a quiet, speculative silence in the room as everyone waited for the rider to approach. You never knew in country like this, what kind of thing was happening to bring a rider in, lickety-spit; usually something bad.

But there were no shouts of alarm or any untoward disturbance as the unseen rider hauled up outside the cantiña.

Everyone there heard the man's boots hit earth as he leaped from the saddle. They heard, too, the soft clink of bridle chains as reins were hitched to the rack.

'A Mex,' Jeff said shrewdly, 'judgin' by the way he left the saddle!'

Phil nodded and smiled at Maria who was standing a few feet away. Then, gazes shuttled to the doors as they were shoved inwards to reveal the figure of a gaily dressed Mexican, even though his concho-decorated bolero and skin-tight pants were powdered with trail-dust. He was big for a Mex and the sugar loaf hat added another fourteen inches to his height. His clothes were plum-coloured except for the white silk shirt and black neckerchief.

Around his slim hips were crossed shell-belts, a gun-filled holster on each side.

Maria and Crockett must have both noticed the long knife scar at almost the same moment. Their gazes swung together, briefly and then returned to the Mexican, on whose brown face was a brash smile of confidence.

But in that brief interchange of glances between Crockett and the girl, there had been the same thought, *this was the bandido who had escaped back into the Eagle Tails, leaving his dead compadre behind!*

CHAPTER 9

JUAN RAMON ESTENADA DIES!

There was a tenseness now in that big room which communicated itself to everyone in turn, even in the space of a few moments. It was as though individual sticks of dynamite were being touched off one after another by a fast travelling trickle of burning powder. Except that there were no deafening explosions; merely that as each man felt the touch of that invisible and insubstantial fuse of tension his head came up and his gaze swivelled from Crockett's loose, relaxed figure, to the gaudily-dressed newcomer; only men's eyes moved, bright with speculation and then this thing communicated itself to the Mex as he hauled up some ten-twelve yards from Crockett and the bar and felt the solid impact of that taut and building silence.

For a thoughtflash, Crockett's mind, or the half of it that was not vitally concerned with absorbing the Mexican's reactions, examined the possibilities as to why one of Vicente's men should suddenly appear in town and boldly enter El Cuchillo for a drink. Then he remembered. None of Vicente's gang had ever been identified according to Maria and Frank Peck. It meant that this bandido should have been safe to show himself openly, *except for that fight in the foot-hills of the Eagle Tails!* How could this outlaw know that the only two people who could identify him were even now in this very room?

From the corner of his eye, Crockett was aware of the pale blur that was Maria's face; he heard the soft rustle of her dress as she moved even while he watched the Mexican's eyes register their sudden and wicked purpose.

Crockett came as near death then, as he had ever done when skirmishing at close quarter with Apaches. For Lieutenant Phil Crockett of the U.S. Cavalry was no lightning draw gun-artist. In army fighting it was covering fire, steady and accurate and continuous shooting; these were the things that counted far above a fast draw. Moreover the Colt in Crockett's sagging holster was of an unfamiliar weight and balance and he was expecting this knife-scarred Mex to dive for one or both of the big guns at his hips.

Juan Ramon Estenada smiled now. A quick, thin, fleeting smile which caused the knife-scar to crease and whiten against the saddle-leather darkness of his skin. He felt more assured now that he knew the man ahead was the one they had met up with some twenty miles from Vicente's camp. Had not his compadre's bullet creased the scalp of this too inquisitive gringo, and would not Juan Ramon Estenada have finished him off completely had it not been for that black-clad sharp-shooter with the so big bore rifle?

Estenada's right hand moved with the speed of a striking rattler as Crockett, half-crouched now, dived for his gun, moments after the Mex's hand had flashed.

'El Cuchillo!' It was Maria's distraught scream which penetrated Crockett's thick cloak of sweaty intentness and in that infinitesimal space of time, so short as to be almost immeasurable, the Spanish word for knife flicked into Crockett's brain with the whirling speed of the weapon itself.

He should have known better than to have expected a Mex to dive for a six-gun; a Mex with a knife-scar running the length of his cheek! He knew as well as Maria or Esteban, or anyone else in this border country, that a Mexican knife artist carried his two-edged weapon in a scabbard suspended between his shoulder blades by means of a cord around his neck. It was this first flashing move *upwards* of the Mexican's right hand which had momentarily thrown Crockett mentally off-balance.

He was half on his knees now, one leg thrust behind him, the Walker Colt out and the hammer thrust back, when the wicked blade hissed through the air, arcing downwards slightly in a perfect parabola as though the Mex had divined his adversary's intention. But the crashing thud, as the knife buried itself into the counter, even as Crockett's gun roared, told its own stark story of success and fortune. It was the first and last time that Estenada had failed and he knew it only too well in that fraction of time between living and dying. The hammer of Crockett's Colt was already drawn back for a second shot, as he crouched tense and immobile, save for the quick beating of his pulse and the trickling sweat down his face.

Powder-smoke drifted lazily upwards to the hanging lamps and threw down its sharp, acrid smell as Juan Ramon Estenada's eyes glazed over and the Mexican's body crashed to the hard-packed floor.

Slowly Crockett regained his feet as the room suddenly exploded into a babble of noise and activity. The batwing doors opened as passers-by, attracted by that single deafening shot, moved in to enjoy the excitement of a fight, maybe a killing. It was quickly evident from the rigidly sprawled figure of the Mex that there had indeed been a killing, and men's glances shuttled towards the drifting cow-poke who was even now only just re-holstering the smoking gun.

Jeff, behind the bar, murmured something softly in Spanish. It might have been a prayer. He grinned and called to Crockett, sloshing whisky into the shot-glass. Phil's glance came round and met Maria's dark, lustrous eyes. Again he saw relief swim in those violet-blue pools, blackly dark against the whiteness of her face.

Men were talking now and Crockett was vaguely conscious of half-heard sentences. '...fair enough fight...', '...thet durned greaser sure asked fer it!' 'Yep! Reckon it was a close call fer Crockett. Why, he scarce had his gun out when the greaser threw!' Another commotion at the doors heralded the arrival of a dark-faced Web Skogee. His black eyes darted every way as he took in the scene – the dead Mex and the very much alive 'cow-poke.'

His bruised and blotched face darkened still further with the anger that was on him and fast pushing him to the breaking point of explosive violence. He half-drew his gun as he held Crockett with his hard stare, but one of the men at the tables spoke. 'Hold et, Web. The cow-poke only shot in self-defence. Yore trouble-maker is right there by yore boots an' by God he won't make no more trouble this side of heaven!'

'That's right, Skogee,' Jeff put in. His voice

was soft and cold and flat. Skogee had never heard it quite like that before.

'What Jim says is true enough. We-all saw it. The greaser went for his knife. It was dam' near stuck in Crockett's gizzard before he even pulled a gun!'

'Eet ees true, Señor Skogee,' Maria confirmed with a brittle smile which did not reach her eyes, ''Ow many weetness would you like? Five, ten, twen'y?' Skogee scowled round at the assembled company, slowly withdrawing his hand from his gun. For once in his lifetime he didn't quite know what to say; anger screwed his words into a tight wad blocking his throat.

'What's up here?' It was Frank Peck's soft, fat voice which now made itself heard through the renewed babble of talk. Skogee wheeled round, grateful for the interruption caused by the sheriff's arrival. Explanations were quickly made and it was pretty clear to Peck that the man Crockett was in the clear by a hundred miles. Maria Cordoba herself spoke for him and her account was substantiated by Jeff's version and several others, notably the three men who had been drinking at the table. Somehow or another, Esteban had appeared, and was watching the scene and the principal actor with his hard, bright eyes.

Crockett's glance was on Skogee's anger-stained face as the deputy looked down at

133

the dead Mex and tried hard to cover up his sudden start of recognition. It confirmed Phil's suspicions, if, indeed, confirmation were needed, that Skogee was tied-in, somehow, with Vicente and his men. He knew this dead Mexican and, judging by the hate and fury in Skogee's eyes, he was not at all pleased with the way events were shaping themselves. Crockett made a further mental note to watch out more than ever for this so-called lawman!...

Crockett wondered as he rose from his cot in the room above the saloon, whether this killing of another member of Vicente's gang would have any effect on the Mexican leader's plans, whatever they were.

Phil washed and shaved, regarding his reflection in the mirror above the wash-stand, with unseeing eyes. By now the news of the army detail would have spread to all interested parties throughout the country and Phil felt reasonably certain that Vicente Tularez, having heard, was not the sort of man to pass up the chance of netting a few more thousand dollars, even though he had lost a couple of his men quite recently.

It might make Tularez a little more wary, of course. He might even wonder whether the Mex who had died in Hondo Bend had talked before cashing in his chips. But there were two aspects about Vicente and his gang which might make for the man's over-confidence. One was the fact that he had a sizeable number of outlaws in his band, perhaps nearly a score or so. Secondly, he had been raiding throughout Maricopa for quite a while and not once, except perhaps at Hondo Bend's bank, had he or his men come anywhere near to being caught. The hold-ups were always carefully organized and the get-aways well planned.

These things considered, Crockett was still sure that once Vicente had decided to go for the 'thinly escorted' paymaster's detail, he would not change his plans on account of one member failing to show up.

Finished dressing, Crockett made for the door, hauling up abruptly as his eye caught sight of the gun-belt and holstered Colt hanging from the back of a chair.

His mind flashed back to last night and perhaps for the first time, now, he realized how lucky he had been. *Lucky that in a house of friends he had been wearing his gun!*

He considered now, with a cold feeling in his stomach, what would undoubtedly have happened had he not been armed. The Mex would have made his throw, just as he had done, and maybe Crockett would have dived, split-second timing saving his life by seconds. But, if he had not had the gun, the Mex, failing to pin Crockett with his knife, would have immediately brought his own guns into play. Jeff would never have had time to slip Crockett the bar shot-gun, nor would Maria have had any opportunity to intervene.

Phil thought of all this grimly and reached out for the gun-belt, buckling it around his lean hips, before descending the stairs to the dining-room and taking his breakfast.

He saw no sign of Maria this morning, and presently, with a restless mood riding him, he stepped out onto the walk, surveying the town in the brilliance and warmth of the early morning.

He had lingered somewhat over his breakfast and afterwards smoked a cigar right down, so that he judged the time now as being a little before eight.

On a sudden impulse, he swung down from the walk and slowly cut across Main at an oblique angle towards the small side street which led to the Shalless cottage. He figured it was not too early to make a social call in a town where stores and saloons mostly opened at eight in the morning. Even now, a few sun-bonneted women were abroad with shopping baskets, anxious to make their purchases before the sun got much hotter.

He found himself outside the cottage in a surprisingly short space of time. The outer door was open to the morning air, so that Crockett unlatched the screen door and stepped inside and into the kitchen-parlour.

Lucy was at the stove, turning quickly as she heard his step and the screen door being opened.

The smile died on her lips as Crockett came in, removing his hat with a murmured, 'Buenos dias.'

He saw the swift change in her face as the warmth and welcome vanished. Her eyes were wide and hostile, her face tightening with something that was even stronger than displeasure.

Crockett was mystified. He stood awkwardly by the table, unwilling to retreat, unconscious of what this was all about. He waited for her to extend the customary invitation and slowly, reluctantly, she offered him coffee.

He thanked her, placing his hat carefully on a chair, wondering whether the preacher were out or still in bed; speculating on the cause of Lucy's frigid reception.

She brought the cup of coffee over to the table, indicating that Crockett should be seated, with a slight movement of her hand.

He said: 'Maybe I didn't come to the meeting on Wednesday, Lucy, and maybe I shall be too busy on Sunday–'

She stormed at him then. Her previous silence all the more marked by contrast with the anger bubbling in her words as they poured from her lips.

'You have a nerve, Mr. Crockett! Coming here and – and – *demanding* the customary hospitality! Expecting decent folks to speak to you and, yes, perhaps even admire you for the wicked thing you have done! No! Don't interrupt me! How dare you come to this house, this place which is dedicated to God, Mr. Crockett, with blood on your hands? Yes! Blood, I say; the blood of a man killed by you.

'Oh yes!' she hurried on, scarcely pausing for breath. 'It only happened last night, but news travels fast in towns such as this. Perhaps you do not consider it murder to kill a Mexican? Perhaps you figure like so many Americanos that the man was just another damned greaser!'

In her wild and distraught frame of mind, Lucy Shalless even used a word which had never before passed her lips.

'Maybe the law, such as it is, condones what you have done, pats you on the back and says, "thank you, Mr. Crockett, for killing another Mex–"'

'Hey! Wait a minute,' Phil said, managing only then to get his protest through the girl's solid wall of vituperation. 'Maybe you *have* heard I killed a Mex last night; news sure *does* travel fast around here. But it was self-defence–'

'*Self-defence!*' There was a world of scorn in her voice as she spat the words out. 'The fact that you saved me the other night from an – er – unpleasant situation–'

'I'm not bringing that up,' Crockett interrupted quietly, though anger and irritation were quickly building up inside him. 'What happened outside the chapel between Skogee and me has nothing to do with this thing. Neither would I attempt to trade on that, Miss Shalless, in order to improve my acquaintance with you! But it sure amazes me that an American woman, such as yourself, who has spent all her life in tough border towns and meeting up with rough-and-tumble men, should–'

'A killing's a killing!' she interrupted him, but now her voice was lower pitched and the flush of anger was receding from her cheeks as though chased away by a retarded sense of justice.

'Oh, I'm sorry I have spoken to you like this, Mr. Crockett. There is no excuse for me losing my temper. We are all poor, weak mortals, devoid of real spiritual values.' She sank into her father's vacant chair and passed a hand wearily over her forehead. 'I guess we look at things from a different angle, I and my father and most other people.'

Crockett stared at her. Anger had suddenly given way to amazement. Almost, he felt an insane desire to laugh.

'Would you have had me stand up like a

dummy in a shooting booth, for the Mex to empty his gun into my belly after he had thrown his cuchillo? And did you know that the man was one of Vicente's gang, with a price on his head and meat for any bounty hunter's or lawman's gun?'

Her eyes widened at this. Here was something new which demanded careful assessment and analysis. But her mind was in conflict, as it always was on such occasions. The insidious doubt again crept into her conscience, as it had done more than once before, that perhaps her father–

Seward Shalless appeared then, descending the stairs, his gaze no longer vague but tightly riveted to Crockett's face.

'If my daughter has not already told you of my wishes, Mr. Crockett,' he proclaimed in his reedy voice, 'let it be known now that we do not welcome gunmen and killers to this house. In future, you will refrain from entering into any kind of communication either with my daughter or myself. We are tolerant people, Mr. Crockett, in a violent land, but even as Jesus scourged the money-lenders from the temple so we scourge the evil-doer and killer.' He paused briefly, one thin, bony hand resting lightly on the table. 'You are no longer welcome here, sir!'

Crockett rose from the table. He had his temper under control now. He gazed almost pityingly at this thin-faced ascetic, so that the spots of colour visible above the golden beard glowed more brightly. Phil even smiled as he stooped to pick up his hat from the chair.

'I fancy that both your daughter and yourself, Shalless, have made your meaning amply clear even to the meanest of intelligences!'

'Wait, Mr. Crockett,' Lucy called sharply as he made for the door. 'You cannot go like this–'

'I can,' Phil contradicted her with a smile. 'What's more, it will save me the bother of thinking up more excuses as to why I haven't attended service. You see, Lucy, I'm just a heathen who'll never be converted!' He could not help that parting shot and even felt momentarily pleased as he saw the girl wince.

He came out onto the gravel path and walked quickly towards El Cuchillo. *The hell with it,* he thought, *I need a drink!*

Then the gun blasted suddenly and from nowhere, echoing across the narrow confines of this small side street. Crockett felt the hot sting as the slug scorched his arm and burned itself through his shirt sleeve. He was instantly awake to the danger and even as he contrived to fall he swore softly that he had allowed himself to be taken again and this in broad daylight. He was flat now, on the hard-packed, rutted road, lying still as though Death were squatted on his shoulders. He did not think the ambusher would try another shot. It was too risky. Already a distant voice was raised on Main and from the corner of his eye Crockett glimpsed the swift movement of a man's booted feet, beyond the palings of a 'dobe house, some thirty yards away. Foliage screened the man's body from Crockett's narrowed gaze, but even at that distance he had caught sight of that one broken spur wheel and knew beyond any doubt that Web Skogee had made his first dry-gulching attack on him!

And, as he lay there, Crockett sent up a silent prayer of thanks to Providence for once again saving him; a prayer as sincere as any murmured by the faithful in the little tin chapel down the street...

CHAPTER 10

DETAIL FROM PHOENIX

Today was Saturday and from the moment of awakening, Crockett had experienced that pleasantly anticipatory feeling which, with him, always preceded action.

The annoyance and irritation caused by the extreme behaviour of Lucy and Seward Shalless now seemed less than a pin-prick. He could afford to laugh at, and even pity this one-sided and unobjective thinking. Even the fact that Web Skogee had tried to shoot him down from ambush, was a thing which now had no power to anger him. Yet Crockett, in his certain knowledge of Skogee's guilt both with regard to the attack and his connection with Vicente's gang, was all the more quietly resolved to settle accounts with the deputy when the time came.

If Vicente's men had gunned down the detail last month, killing Cass Cherry, *then it had been because of information which Skogee had supplied to the Mexican bandido!* Of that Crockett was sure and the knowledge imbued in him a cold, quiet determination rather than any wild upsurge of anger…

Later, in the evening, in Maria's private parlour at the rear, Crockett told the girl what had happened the preceding day.

Maria Cordoba's eyes darkened with anger as she listened.

'Eet ees a crazy theeng, Señor Pheel, when a man, or a woman, cannot onderstan' the deef-rence between murder an' self-defence!'

Crockett nodded and gave a wry grin. 'I'm not altogether surprised at the preacher, but I figured Lucy had more horse sense than that.'

Maria said: 'Eet ees all the more deeficult for a man of action to 'ave to put weeth thees theengs; and the waiting. Soon now, you will be moving again, like you were commanding a detail. Tomorrow, you weel 'ave a hoss under you and weel be weeth your friends!'

'My army friends, yes,' Crockett replied soberly. 'But I am not forgetful of the fact that if I have enemies in Hondo Bend, I also have some good friends. You, Esteban, Jeff! How would I have made out without your help, Maria? I'd have been buzzard meat for sure, and once that had happened and the facts were made known, no other soldier would have been allowed to carry on. Cass Cherry would never be avenged!'

'I onderstan',' Maria said, moving across

to the long windows overlooking the darkened patio. 'By tomorrow you weel be on your way, Pheel, an' eef you succeed in trapping Vicente then, I guess I – 'Ondo Bend weel not see you some more!'

Crockett's glance moved over to the girl as she stood with her back to him, rapier straight. He noticed now that she wore a plum-coloured velvet dress – en cuerpo, save for where it billowed out from the waist and reached to the high-heeled matching slippers. A silver belt of early Spanish or even Aztec work, perhaps, encircled the slim waist. The gleaming black hair was parted in the middle and was softly gathered back to the nape of the neck and held by a single silver ribbon.

He had scarcely realized to the full her startling beauty, and today, somehow, it seemed more vivid, more apparent than hitherto. Admiration was in Crockett's eyes, not only for the physical, but for the unseen, inner qualities which this woman had shown so repeatedly during his short time in Hondo Bend and El Cuchillo in particular.

'You're not often wrong, Maria,' he told her quietly, 'but if you figure I won't be coming to Hondo Bend again, you mak' the beeg mistake!'

His tone was half-serious, half-bantering, and now he lit a cigar with a burning twig from the stone fireplace. 'I've found a place now where I can spend the odd leave days and nights, Maria. Remember? It's called El Cuchillo! Apart from that, there may be "business" which might well bring me back here. Web Skogee, for instance. Whatever the outcome of the next few days, whatever happens to Vicente and his gang, the business between me and Skogee is now something personal! I've got no *proof* that he's tied-in with Tularez, same as I've got no proof it was he who made that dry-gulching attack–'

She turned now and there was the suggestion of a smile parting her soft red lips. She was too far away for Crockett to see the dew-like sparkle of wetness in her eyes...

Lieutenant Giff Martin was a straight-backed young Academy officer who took his duties with a scrupulous conscientiousness which at times barely left room for the humour that lay deep down inside the man. He did not quite possess the relaxed assurance, nor the easy-going yet disciplined mind of his senior officer, Lieutenant Phil Crockett, yet there was a comradeship existing between these two men, not altogether surprising.

Whilst there were several qualities in Crockett which Giff Martin quietly condemned in his own mind, there were others too, the kind that cause a man to rise in his stirrups and make his charge against over-whelming odds when the breath of battle and sudden death is blowing on his cheeks. Giff knew there was no fear in Crockett and nothing the man would not do, if called upon. That was the kind of trait on which, like a corner stone, the bricks of loyalty and admiration would be firmly lodged. If Crockett were a little too easy going with enlisted men, Giff Martin had to admit, even whilst he deplored such an attitude, that Crockett got better results from the men of 'C' Troop than did any other officer from his own particular company.

Giff smiled briefly as he thought of these things and switched his mind back to the present. A hundred yards down street Hondo Bend lay, a mass of night-enveloped 'dobe and clap-board buildings with their winking eyes of bright chrome. The faintest glow of refracted lamp-light rainbowed the small town with the soft irridescence of an all but invisible halo.

Giff Martin's mouth twisted wryly as he considered the inappropriateness of such a simile!

'Sergeant!' he called, turning in the saddle to Bryne Ewart. 'Find a suitable vacant lot and tell Trooper Jones to drive the wagon onto it. Mount a constant guard. There must be no less than three men awake and on guard at all times throughout the night, and see that the horses are cared for.'

'Very good, sir,' Ewart replied, and bringing his horse in closer, lowered his voice. 'You'll find the lieutenant in El Cuchillo, sir. Like I said, the woman and her mozo can both be trusted.'

Giff Martin nodded. He didn't like this bit about a Spanish woman and a Mex mozo being involved in a secret Army job, but if Crockett had considered it expedient – he shrugged and put his horse towards Main and El Cuchillo.

Giff dismounted at the rack in front of the cantiña and stiffened suddenly as he heard his name softly called from the shadows of the 'dobe wall adjoining.

He grinned then, recognizing the voice, and unhurriedly tied the gelding's reins. He gave one slow, casual glance about him before stepping into the pool of shadow and reaching Crockett. Phil's low voice cautioned Martin not to talk as he led the way along the wall and through the iron gate into the patio. Once inside, well away from the street, Crockett turned, grinned and shook Giff Martin's gloved hand.

'Good to see you, Giff. How's everything?'

Martin smiled and said, 'Okay, Phil,' cautiously. 'Can't we go up to your room, I'm not sure of talking with all these walls and shadows?'

'We can do better than that, Giff,' Phil said, leading the way through the patio door and veering from the corridor into Maria's private parlour.

He turned up the lamps and Giff Martin had his long and surprised look at the exquisitely furnished room.

'Who'd have thought a place could be furnished like this in a town such as Hondo Bend?'

Crockett smiled, selected two cigars and handed one to Martin. When the smokes were drawing, Crockett said, 'What's the plan, Giff, or do I know?'

Martin chose a chair near the fireplace, sitting on the extreme edge, conscious that his uniform and boots were trail-dusty.

'Sergeant Ewart met up with us somewhere between here and Phoenix, Phil. He told me more or less what had happened whilst I was taking the detail by a round-about route.

'We take out tomorrow early and meet up with Sergeant Emery and the twenty troopers at a dip in the trail which is almost completely hidden from the rest of the country. Once the men are safely in the wagon we carry on towards the fort. Each night the undercover troopers will stay inside or under the wagon. We go on like that until something happens.'

Crockett nodded. 'My guess, Giff, is that

the trouble will be at Hondo Bend itself, where the river doubles back and probably near where they held up the wagon before. It's a natural spot for an ambush...'

Martin grinned. 'I sure hope they do, Phil. This time we'll give them hell! Anything else on your mind?'

'Yes. One thing. Tomorrow early, I'll be at the cantiña's bar, and I'll ask you for permission to ride with your detail to the fort.'

'That, of course, will be for the benefit of anyone listening, particularly if they are in cahoots with Vicente?'

'Sure,' Crockett murmured, 'though I'm pretty sure I know who it is and I'm hoping that my own personal feud won't upset Vicente's plans.'

Crockett went on to tell his fellow lieutenant about Web Skogee, their fight and Skogee's ultimate bushwhacking attempt.

Martin's eyes widened. 'And you're complaining of sitting here being *idle*?' he said with a grin. 'It seems to me, Phil, you've been spending a deal of time fighting everyone single-handed in between having your wounds attended to by this saloon girl!'

Crockett flushed; he knew that Giff had spoken in all innocence, not knowing what Maria was like; not having met her and, therefore, putting his own interpretation on the Spanish girl according to his own

Boston Society level. There were two kinds of women as conceived by Giff Martin's standards. The kind a man married and the kind he didn't. A man did not marry a saloon girl or the proprietress of a near Mex cantiña even though he might have some quiet and discreet fun...

'Let me disabuse your mind at once, Giff,' Crockett said feeling oddly strong about this, of a sudden.

'Maria Cordoba is neither a saloon girl, a camp follower, a harlot, or any other such thing as you have already tagged her in your mind. She–'

Martin was profuse in his apologies, blushing hotly. 'I'm sorry, Phil. I meant no harm. I take that back–'

He started slightly and turned, letting his words trail off into nothing. The door had opened and a woman stood there, pausing for a moment before stepping into the room and closing the door softly behind her. A woman dressed en cuerpo in plum-covered velvet; raven black hair drawn back; dark violet eyes fixed soberly on Giff Martin's face. He managed to get to his feet, his gaze shuttling back to Crockett's face. There was amazed speculation in Giff's wide eyes; disbelief; incredulity.

Crockett smiled. 'May I present Lieutenant Giff Martin, Maria, of Fort Yuma? Giff, this is Maria de Mendoza y Cordoba,

151

late of Mexico and now owner of El Cuchillo!'

She flashed Crockett a quick glance. *How has he learned my full name?* she wondered.

But Martin fairly goggled, though his upbringing was too strongly rooted for him to forget himself entirely.

He stepped forward, taking Maria's hand and bowing low, and for sheer gallantry any Boston beau would have seemed gauche and callow by comparison.

'Any friend of the Señor Crockett ees my friend also,' Maria said. 'I know that eet ees often said with the tongue but not weet' the heart. My casa is yours,' she finished simply, extending to Crockett's fellow officer the greatest hospitality and compliment that any Spaniard can pay.

'Your servant, ma'am,' Martin said with a quick, deep sincerity. He gazed into her eyes as he released her hand and knew that what Crockett had told him was the simple truth.

'I guess we're already indebted to you, ma'am,' Giff said, having recovered himself. 'It appears that Phil would have been buzzard meat but for your timely inter-vention and nursing, more than once!'

Maria smiled. 'I theenk we should drink a toast to the success of your plan. You weel take some tequila weeth me? Tomorrow there weel be so leetle time!'...

Dust rose lazily above and behind the small, slow-moving cavalcade. Ahead of the paymaster's wagon Sergeant Bryne Ewart rode, blue eyes alert and sweeping the distant buttes. Lieutenant Martin kept his mount alongside the canvas-topped wagon, whilst four mounted troopers and a drifting cow-poke brought up the rear.

The sun climbed higher, investing the land and everything on it with its burning heat. By the middle of the forenoon the detail had moved down into the dip. Ahead of Crockett and the four raw-boned troopers, the wagon came to a halt and from the boulders and rocks and scrub south of the main river, a score of blue-clad, sweating troopers slithered out from their hiding place, like an army of dark blue lizards. Each man clutched a Springfield carbine as he now ran forward stooping low until reaching the wagon. Within the space of five minutes the detail was moving on again, a thinly escorted pay-wagon with no outward indication that underneath the white canvas top twenty picked skirmishers were crouching, rifles held upthrust between knees, in a grim, sweaty silence.

Crockett, observing the smoothness of the operation allowed himself a momentary feeling of admiration before putting his glasses to the surrounding country, particularly the rim-rock ahead where the river and the thin trail itself narrowed and quartered through the canyon-like escarpment where the Hondo flowed into the mother river and from which place the town of Hondo Bend derived its name.

Here the trail swung away a little, south of the actual confluence of the river and its tributary. During the Spring rains the ford would be difficult or impossible to negotiate, but now, levels were already lowering fast, and the trick was merely to negotiate the two grades of the Hondo's banks.

Sergeant Ewart put his horse to the river, finding the gravel-bottomed fording place and hitting the opposite bank after no more than a few minutes in the slow-moving water. He pulled in at the river's edge, signalling the wagon to come up and make the crossing. Behind, as closely as possible, Lieutenant Giff Martin and Crockett and the four troopers rode in a tight bunch.

It was an anxious few moments, yet neither Crockett nor Martin considered an attack here as being likely. The rocky slopes, though jagged and saw-toothed on either side, were too low to afford much cover for an ambush party. It was further on that the trouble, if any, could be expected, where scrub-covered talus slopes and rim-rock shouldered their way upwards above the river and trail, walling in the detail as it moved steadily forward, every man's eyes alert and searching, gauntleted right hands free and ready to reach for guns.

Crockett found that he was sweating now and realized grimly that it was not entirely due to the sun's noon heat. From time to time, Martin's glance swept upwards to the oven-hot rocks, towering above; then his glance shuttled back to Crockett's set face.

The iron-tyred wheels of the wagon threw off sparks as they rolled on and over the rock-strewn trail. The sound was a steady, grinding noise in the midday heat, punctuated only by the sharp ring of iron-shod hoofs, the squeak of saddle leather and the soft jingle of bridle-chains and accoutrements.

No one spoke. There was nothing to say. Only men's gazes, sharp and probing, reflected the building tension inside each trooper.

They had almost reached the half-way mark where the high canyon walls began their steep descent to flatten out again and lose themselves in brush and grass along the river bottom.

Giff Martin wiped his face with the yellow kerchief at his neck, and it was almost as though that simple, everyday action had been a signal for the long-awaited climax.

Another quarter-mile onwards and the detail would have been well clear and away from the worst part of the narrow trail. As it was, prepared though they all were, there was still the shock of surprise when it came, in the shape of a huge boulder, loosened and set in motion from the top of the rim-rock...

CHAPTER 11

HOLD-UP AT HONDO BEND

Trooper Jones, on the wagon seat, lifted his eyes as he saw and heard the huge rock hurtling downwards. He sawed mightily on the reins, trying hard to turn the wagon horses about in a tight circle. He got them only halfway round, impeded as he was by the narrowness of the trail here and the rock-strewn terrain.

Crockett shouted his warning then as his hand dived towards the carbine on his saddle. He ordered the men to dismount and for a horse-holder to take up the reins. Sergeant Ewart was already out of the saddle, throwing the reins to the trooper who came running up. Above him, on the very pinnacle of the rim-rock, Crockett had his first glimpse of the Chihuahua hats as he slid from leather.

The boulder came down, crashing into the wagon horses with a terrific impact and speed. Jones had been unable to pull the vehicle out of the path of destruction.

The near-side horse went down, a mass of crushed bone and flesh. The three remaining horses threw up and squealed sharply in their terror, but the traces held for the moment, so that they were pinned fast by the rock lodged against the mangled horse.

Already the troopers had spewed out of the wagon at the first sound of trouble. They were no longer sweaty with anxiety but were coolly placing their shots upwards at the same time seeking whatever cover afforded.

For a few moments the crash of gunfire was an almost continuous cannonade. The thunder of the Springfields and Crockett's Winchester rolled along the walls of rock. Guns spoke from above and lead screamed down into and around the empty wagon, sometimes ricocheting sharply from stones or the iron-bound wheels.

If it were difficult for the troopers to aim upwards at the all but invisible figures of the bandidos, it was not much easier for Vicente's men to shoot downwards with any degree of accuracy unless they were to stand up and reveal themselves completely.

Crockett put his quick gaze to the scene along the trail. He saw that there was now no trooper without some kind of rock or boulder behind which he sheltered and from where he continued to pump lead upwards. The horse-holder had done a good job in getting the scared geldings away from the line of fire. One horse was gone down, but the man had fought grimly to maintain his hold on the reins and had eventually contrived to lead them to comparative safety. Crockett's quick mental note of this, even in the heat of battle, would bring its reward to that trooper.

But worse was to come. Evidently, Vicente was not content to sit and fight this thing out. It could be a stalemate perhaps, with one of the troopers galloping away for reinforcements.

Vicente Tularez looked down on the scene from a safe distance and lifted his arm in a signal...

Crockett saw the small, bounding package-like object without at first realizing what it was.

It came at a seemingly slow-moving speed, once or twice rebounding from the tips of rocks but still heading straight for the wagon and the skirmishers spread out and around and behind.

Crockett stood erect now, his gun empty and unmindful of the screaming lead which Vicente's band was still throwing downwards in a fiercer fusillade than ever. A warning voice was shouting in Crockett's mind, so that, momentarily, the roar of battle faded away.

He saw the spluttering fuse which still burned in spite of the thing's rough descent over the rocks. He ran forward shouting to the men as he ran, bullets chipping away the rocks at his feet and zinging angrily in all directions. One bullet caught his boot-heel, causing him to stumble and fall. He got up again quickly, bruised and shaken. His hand reached out for the package – a dozen or so sticks of dynamite tightly tied together. The fuse was down to an inch and burning fiercely.

Crockett caught hold of the home-made bomb and instead of stamping out the fuse ran back a few paces from the wall of rock. He was now in full view of the nearest of the bandidos who, seeing him thus exposed, started in to mow him down. But, instantly, Giff Martin's voice rose cool, yet penetrating above the din. 'Rapid fire, men! Cover Lieutenant Crockett. By God–'

His voice was drowned in the sudden concerted roar of a score of carbines, each man risking showing himself a little in order to aim upwards at the bobbing heads and shoulders amongst the rocks. Vicente's men had no chance to cut Crockett down with this kind of fire in their faces. More than one shrill scream echoed downwards amongst the lower rocks and became lost in a rolling thunder of a second volley.

But Crockett had not stood out there for very long, even though, to Giff Martin, it had seemed an eternity. Phil had stayed still no longer than it had taken him to retrieve the 'bomb' and hurl it upwards with all his might. So terrific had been that throw, through the necessity to make certain the dynamite did not rebound and come back, that for a moment, Crockett found his right arm hanging uselessly. The pain in his shoulder told him that the ball was dislodged from its socket. His face was grey with dust and pain, and sweat ran down making rivers in the mask of dirt covering his lean face. He had almost forgotten about the dynamite until a loud explosion reached his ears and, instinctively he half-ran, half-threw himself forward nearer in to the base of the towering wall.

Each man behind him, thanks to Giff Martin's shouted warning, had likewise flattened himself in the earth behind his own particular shelter. Small fragments of rock rose sharply and viciously into the air. One or two medium-sized rocks came tumbling down to land on the narrow trail. But the major amount of damage had occurred above, among Vicente's own men. Screams like the tormenting of lost souls, floated downwards. Dust and rubble slowly settled as troopers picked themselves up, giving wry grins as they found themselves still in one piece. Over to the wagon, Trooper Jones lay stretched out, on his face, unmoving. Farther away, Sergeant Bryne Ewart sat back against a rock, white of face and bloody of arm and swearing softly.

161

Crockett got to his feet, standing shakily in the cover of the overhanging rock, as Martin ran forward, Colt revolver in his right hand.

'You're hurt, Phil!' he rasped, breathing heavily with his exertions. 'What you want us to do, winkle them out?'

Crockett nodded. 'Hold a couple of men to cover the rest as they move up. Hell! Giff, you don't have to be told. Play it your way. I guess we've got them on the run!'

Martin nodded, his eyes expressing a grateful approval. 'I'll send McCleary over to you to get that arm back.'

He turned and ran back to the men, issuing his terse orders.

In pain Crockett watched whilst the skirmishers fanned out and approached the rock-wall under cover of three troopers blazing away with the carbines. There seemed to be little firing from above. The initiative was now with the army!

Fury, born of the knowledge that this raid had been a costly failure both in money and men, held Vicente Tularez in its rigid grip.

From time to time he glanced at the hawk-like face of Ramirez as the two men rode hard, stirrup to stirrup away from the scene of slaughter at Hondo Bend.

This was to have been the biggest thing ever, Tularez gritted as he thought back on Web Skogee's message. The deputy had

162

assured him that not only would the pay-wagon be carrying more dinero than usual but that the whole escort would not amount to more than five-six armed troopers.

Right up until the time when Tularez had signalled for the throwing of the 'bomb,' an added argument thought up by Ramirez, the bandit leader had felt confident about the outcome even though he had been shocked to observe and hear that many more than five-six carbines were speaking.

He thought back on the scene at Hondo Bend, for a moment, knowing that once decided on the raid, he could scarcely have played it any other way.

The high canyon walls on the far side – the north side of the river – were too far away to make accurate shooting a practical pro-position. Thus Vicente had been forced to group his men all on the one side, south of the river and overlooking the thin trail. It had been a good spot for an ambush and, ordinarily he would have smashed the escort and got away with the money. But something had gone wrong, in spite of Skogee's careful information! Tularez' eyes turned blacker than ever as he considered the possibility that the deputy had deliberately mis-informed him. Tularez became aware then that his lieutenant was pulling his lathered mount to a halt, flashing a backward glance towards the distant rising rim-rock.

'What ees eet, Ramirez?' Vicente rasped. 'We mus' not stop now...'

Ramirez pointed to the white saline deposits on the breasts and forelegs of both their mounts. Even though the horses were of the finest stock in the country, the pace from Hondo Bend had been long and killing.

'We 'ave to rest zee mounts, Vicente,' Ramirez said. 'Zey cannot go on much longer. Look! Yonder ees a wall of rock and a spring. Let us rest an' dreenk!'

Grudgingly, half-fearfully, the fat little renegade acknowledged the truth and wisdom of his lieutenant's advice. They spurred their now drooping mounts towards the wall of rock where Ramirez had remembered a spring trickled through the grey-green scrub. Ahead, but still many miles away, the Eagle Tails lifted towards the afternoon sky. The westering sun threw down its final explosions of heat before dropping down behind the white-capped mountain peaks.

Ramirez, having off-saddled and hobbled the sweating horses, went about the task of gathering brush and enough greasewood for a small fire.

'Eet weel be safe to 'ave thees fire so early, Vicente,' he said, 'but after we 'ave eaten we weel put heem out!'

Tularez nodded and his fat jowls quivered.

It seemed strange that it was Ramirez who now seemed to be taking the initiative and at any other time, Vicente would have asserted himself heavily. Now after the shock of failure, with most of his men lying back there at Hondo Bend, dead or wounded, after that, and the gruelling ride to escape, the outlaw chief seemed suddenly apathetic. Even his anger no longer had the power to hold him stiff and erect and fiercely aggressive.

Ramirez' eyes slid over to where his chief sat, fat chin sunk onto the dirty silk shirt over his breast.

Shortly, Ramirez produced the heated food which was to serve them until they could regain the safety of their camp in the mountain fastness.

Vicente stirred sufficiently to wolf the heavily spiced Mex food. There was also a flask of tequila, Ramirez, old campaigner that he was, never neglecting to keep his saddle-bags well filled even when taking out for a raid. The more so then, in fact, because a man could never be certain but what he would not be chased and have to take circuitous trails and wide-sweeping paths before getting back – if then!

'I weel watch, Vicente,' the indefatigable Ramirez offered presently. 'But we must be off again before the sun she rise!'

With the false dawn having but lately

flared, Ramirez laid down his rifle and kneeling down at the spring, drank first and afterwards sluiced face and hands in the cool water. Presently, with a quick glance at the snoring Tularez, he stepped away from the camp and put his gaze to the desert all around. He could not see much, for as yet there was only the merest tone of paler night in the eastern sky, but Ramirez keened the soft pre-dawn wind and pointed his face towards the river, his nostrils widely flared. It was as though he had the ability to scent out whether or not they were being pursued. Perhaps he had, for, in a short while he returned and kindled a small fire, placing the remains of the frijoles and fumado in a can and suspending it over the coals.

Vicente awoke to the appetizing smell and after eating his share of breakfast, made a pretence of washing at the nearby stream.

'Ees all right, Ramirez?' he asked wiping his face on the neckerchief, his black beady eyes shifting anxiously.

Ramirez nodded. 'They not follow us, I theenk, Vicente. We weel be back to camp soon after noon, but we mus' start prontito!'...

There was no school this Monday morning, the day after the pay-wagon detail had taken out from Hondo Bend accompanied by Pete Crockett. Lucy Shalless had risen earlier

166

than usual. The preacher, in one of his saner moments, had quietly urged his daughter to make another trip to a Mex village, this time north of the river in the twenty-mile valley between the Dame Mountain and the Eagle Tails.

Cal Bellenger had rented her a paint pony and at eight o'clock the animal was ready, bridled, and the side-saddle cinched across its back.

She was glad of this opportunity of riding; of late her thoughts had been troubled. Doubts, which no convert should entertain had beset her and blushingly she had to admit to herself that they were problems mainly concerning men!

Ever since that rather frightening episode outside the chapel on Wednesday night, and later, after Crockett had shot the Mexican in the cantiña her mind had been balanced on the razor edge of doubt as to whether she had accorded the right treatment to Web Skogee and Crockett himself.

Strangely, Lucy had regarded Skogee's 'attack' on her much more tolerantly than she had Crockett's shooting of one of Vicente's gang. To Lucy's tidy mind, as she herself had said, a killing was a killing, and in her simple make-up there was no room for the finer differentiations between murder and self-defence. The fact that Crockett had not only been exonerated but praised

167

by Frank Peck and Holt Caddo, was just another indication of the wickedness and fallacies of these man-made laws!

But now Lucy was wondering whether her treatment had not been over-harsh. After all, she reminded herself, her own religion taught tolerance to the wrong-doer, the wayward and the weak. And now, quite objectively, she realized that she had shown more than a goodly proportion of tolerance to Web Skogee – *because she had wanted to!*

Even though some anger and disgust lingered, she had accepted his abject apology and excuse for the fact that he had been 'drinking overmuch.'

But towards Crockett, as a killer, even though the argument was self-defence, she had maintained an implacable and undeviating attitude of unforgiveness. Even if she *had* sought a reconciliation, her father she reminded herself had forbidden any sort of communication between the two. Thus, with her mind being miserably uncertain, like a child come suddenly face to face with the world, she was more than glad for the opportunity to ride out from town and rest her troubled eyes on this harsh yet savagely beautiful country. The sight of the majestic Eagle Tails lifting to the steel-blue sky, rarely failed to move and hold her, and they did not fail now to take her thoughts away from herself for a little while, even though yesterday morning she had seen Crockett move out to the Fort Yuma trial with the detail and had experienced a surprising and bitter disappointment, figuring that she would not see him again.

Shortly, she lifted the paint's reins and put the animal to the distant cluster of 'dobes and sun-bleached huts which indicated the small village that was her first port of call.

To her left, Dame Mountain pushed its jagged peaked summit to the brassy sky; northwards and shouldering away to the north-west, the Eagle Tails rose from the floor of the valley.

She thought she could just make out Mesa Rock, but she was not quite sure at this distance.

Suddenly, as she rode slowly towards the village, still another two or three miles distant, some instinctive warning sounded inside her causing her to turn in the saddle and survey her back-trail for the first time since leaving Hondo Bend. She saw then the fast moving dust cloud and knew that at least one or two riders were pushing their mounts at a fast and urgent pace.

She gigged her horse over to the grass verge, realizing that the riders would want all of the trail if they were to maintain that killing pace. Even now she was not really scared. It was almost like that Wednesday night, as though Lucy Shalless were incapable of assessing the degrees of wickedness in some men...

She saw them now as two Mexicans, dust covered and gradually easing their mounts to a trot and then a walk. One of them was thin and slight and dark, handsome in a way. The other! Lucy shuddered involuntarily. He was short and fat and gross and his oily face was covered in black stubble as well as sweat and alkali. Drooping moustaches bracketed his mouth and reached almost to his ponderous, wobbly dewlaps.

With a sudden start of surprised dismay, Lucy saw the men pull up and survey her with dark speculative eyes. She had expected that they would no more than touch the floppy brims of their Chihuahua hats, pass the time of day, and then spur on to the village ahead.

Instead they put their eyes on her in a way that a man might judge a piece of horse-flesh or a steer. She suddenly felt herself go hot all over. Scarlet stained her cheeks, yet her gaze held unflinchingly to those two pairs of bold, black and calculating eyes.

CHAPTER 12

SHERIFF'S POSSE

It was the gross-looking fat man who spoke first, talking in Spanish, which Lucy Shalless understood and spoke perfectly.

'Not only dollars, perhaps, Ramirez, but safety as well, eh?'

Ramirez smiled insolently. 'If you are thinking as I am, mio Encomendero, it would be a smart trick, as the Americanos would say. A snatch, huh? Maybe if we hold the girl then the alcalde, even the army, might be more amenable to reason!'

Vicente grinned evilly and nodded. Lucy gazed in fascinated horror as the little Mexican's face quivered like a dirty, chocolate blancmange. For a moment she was tempted to resort to flight, but even as the impulse came, she realized that the paint, after its long journey, would be no match for the big Arab horses which the Mexicans rode so easily. It was already approaching noon, and she had been riding the paint since early morning. True, the Mexicans had been racing their mounts, but the animals though trail-dusty were scarcely blowing and, instinctively, Lucy knew that there would be no hope in flight.

'You weel come quietly to our camp, señorita,' Ramirez asked, 'or do you weesh that we tie you up like zee wild hog?' He hastened to rectify any seeming ungallantry. 'Zee comparison was mos' unfortunate, Señorita Shalless! Please forgeeve me!'

Lucy was of a mind to tell this slight, evilly handsome greaser not to bother with broken English, that she understood Spanish perfectly, but she checked herself in time. It might be a good card to hold up her sleeve...

She spoke quietly and determinedly now, her panic and distress miraculously giving place to an unusual fortitude. 'Kidnapping is a Federal offence,' she said between her teeth. 'But I suppose that means little to so notorious a person as Vicente Tularez!' She watched the outlaw's surprised, half-pleased reaction. It had been a blind guess on Lucy's part, yet the intuitive side of her had been certain that this indeed was the dirty little renegade who had played havoc with stage-coaches, army pay-wagons and, lately, Hondo Bend's Bank. Strangely, she felt little of her former fear now. 'The punishment for kidnapping is death, Vicente,' she said boldly, 'but I cannot resist and you know it. Perhaps if you remember I am a woman and an Americano, and treat me with respect, the penalties will not be so severe!'

172

Tularez laughed, a deep rumbling noise that rose from the depths of his belly. 'Ze señorita ees as funny as she ees brave!' He leaned forward as he spoke, pudgy hands clasped across the horn of his saddle.

'By ze time we feenish, señorita, we not only get ze amnesty but mucho dinero as well!' He laughed again and then suddenly motioned to his lieutenant. Ramirez caught the bridle reins of Lucy's paint, half-hitching them around the horn of his saddle. She was forced now to follow at the slim man's stirrup.

Vicente went into the lead, swinging away from the main trail and taking a brush-choked cut off, so narrow as to preclude the possibility of allowing two riders abreast.

Ramirez quickly substituted his rawhide reata for the reins, tying one end firmly to Lucy's saddle and making a dally on his own rig with the shortened line. This way, they progressed in silence and in heat, mounting steadily, cutting through rim-rock trails and dry gulches, occasionally emerging into the wooded talus slope carpeted with pine needles a million years old and then hitting rock or shale as they moved ever upwards to the higher benched slopes of the Eagle Tails.

Several times during that gruelling ascent, men and horses were forced to rest. During one of these periods, Vicente started questioning the silent, tight-lipped girl.

'Zees man, Crockett, señorita. What do you know of him, huh?'

Lucy said, 'Not much and if I did, I wouldn't tell you if I figured you wanted to know!'

Vicente's mouth tightened so that in spite of the surrounding superfluity of flesh it resembled nothing so much as a steel-trap.

'We 'ave ways of makin' zee mos' obstinate man or woman talk, señorita,' he said softly. 'Ees not zees hombre pairhaps ondaircover marshal?'

Lucy's blue eyes widened in genuine surprise. 'Why, I hadn't thought of it, but maybe you are right and maybe he will be annoyed when he discovers what you have done!'

Yet as she spoke, Lucy's heart sank as she recollected that yesterday Pete Crockett had ridden out of town with the army detail headed for Fort Yuma. If anything in the way of her rescue were to be achieved, it would rest solely on the shoulders of men like Frank Peck, Holt Caddo and Web Skogee. Lucy didn't give much for the chances of a spectacular and dramatic rescue by these lawmen. Why, they hadn't even been able to trail Vicente further than the foothills, let alone find his camp and rescue anyone!

'She weel tell us what she know, pretty

dam' soon,' Ramirez said smiling. 'Once we get back to the camp. Come, Vicente, let us go. Pedro and Arispe weel be expecting us.'

Crockett leaned back in the sparse shade thrown by the high canyon wall at his back. Sweat stood out on his face, glistening like large globules of mercury.

McCleary thrust the bottle towards the lieutenant's dry lips. 'Take another swig, sir, you won't feel it so much with another drink under your belt!'

Crockett drank and allowed the whisky to swim around his dry mouth before swallowing it. Already, the sickening pain in his shoulder was rapidly subsiding. McCleary had got the ball back into the socket before swelling had made it an almost impossible chore.

Crockett's sweat-filled eyes saw Sergeant Bryne Ewart through a haze. 'How's the sergeant's arm, McCleary?' he asked.

'Nothin' to worry over, sir,' McCleary grinned. 'Rock splinters from a ricochet. The sergeant'll be all right in no time.'

Crockett turned his gaze again and saw that even now Bryne Ewart, his arm bandaged, was picking up his carbine and following in the footsteps of the others already scaling the height of the rim-rock.

There were no sounds of shooting and it soon became obvious that there would be no further opposition from Vicente's badly mauled band.

Giff Martin was back within the hour, squatting down on his haunches and making his brief, informal report to Crockett.

'Thanks to you, Phil, there's seven-eight dead greasers up there amongst the rocks and a couple badly wounded who won't last more than a few hours. As to Vicente, he must have high-tailed pretty dam' quick if he was there at all. Anyway, there's no sign of him, but I guess we've smashed his gang all right!'

'Vicente's the most dangerous of the whole outfit, Giff,' Crockett said slowly. 'With him loose, it means I must go back to Hondo Bend. How are your own men, Giff?'

Martin said, 'We came off pretty well, considering. Ewart's arm is not so bad, but Jones is dead and so is Corporal Fallows. Apart from that there are just a few minor wounds.'

Phil nodded. 'We were lucky. That dynamite was a goddam unexpected thing. Now, Giff. You take back to the fort, will you, and report everything that's happened? Tell Mitch I'm returning to Hondo Bend and am likely to be away till we've settled one way or another with Vicente.'

Giff said, 'You'd best watch out for this deputy sheriff hombre you told me about.

He seems to be the nigger in the wood-pile!'

Again Crockett nodded. 'His day of reckoning is not far away, Giff. This is out in the open now. No more undercover stuff. Hondo Bend'll want to know why I've returned and this time they'll have it straight and know I'm an army man. Whatever else,' Crockett added grimly, 'Skogee and Tularez are nearing the end of their ropes...'

McCleary had put Phil's right arm in a sling fashioned from his neckerchief. He was able to rest the dully aching joint as he rode slowly back to town.

Behind him, dust rose to form a yellow, shifting screen, marking the passage of the detail headed for the fort, the strong box intact!

The sun was westering, had almost disappeared from view when Crockett turned onto Hondo Bend's Main. One or two loafers eyed him in mild surprise as he tied the gelding to the rack fronting El Cuchillo. They had not expected to see the Señor Crockett back so soon. Had not he talked of joining the Americano army?

Phil walked tiredly across the broad-walk to the batwing doors, suddenly, surprisingly glad that he was here again and would see Maria.

Jeff looked up from serving drinks, eyeing the newcomer speculatively and then grinning with pleasure as he identified the dust-covered figure of Pete Crockett.

'Step right up, Pete,' he called. 'Four fingers of rye coming up!' He pushed a shot-glass and bottle towards the tired lieutenant and leaned across the bar, speaking softly.

'The señorita's in back, Pete, if you should want?'

Crockett smiled. 'Thanks, Jeff; a drink and a wash-up first, though.'

Phil had wondered how he would play it when he met up with Skogee again. He had probed the possibility of throwing a gun on the deputy and accusing him outright of the attempted bushwhacking and also his complicity in Vicente's lawless activities. Second thoughts, however, on the journey back from the scene of battle, had resulted in a decision to play the thing close to his vest. The time would come, undoubtedly, when Web Skogee would make his wrong move. Then Crockett would jump right onto his neck!

He decided that a wash could wait and, downing his drink, passed through the door leading into the rear corridor. He knocked at the door on the left and Maria's soft, liquid voice bade him enter.

He stood just inside the room, watching her. She did not turn immediately. She was gazing out of the windows on to the patio, as though there were something out there on the flagged path of vital interest to her.

When she did turn, with a gesture half of impatience, saying, 'What is it, Esteban?' Crockett saw the flush stain her cheeks and the lips curve in a smile. He felt the strong, welcoming strike of her eyes as she moved quickly across the room and caught his arm.

'Pheel! Eet ees good to see you again and so soon! What news do you breeng? 'Ow deed eet go? Deed you keel Vicente–?'

Crockett grinned and placed his own hand over hers.

'One at a time, Maria, for heaven's sake. Yes! I reckon you could say the news is good. We pretty well broke up Vicente's gang but he himself escaped. We figure he lit out once again for the Eagle Tails. This time I'm going in there and getting him. He cain't have many men left now, if any!'

'I am so glad you are safe, Pheel,' Maria said presently. 'But I do not lik' you to go and–' She broke off suddenly, biting her lips and Crockett had a moment's realization of something that even now he was not prepared to recognize. But he was saved further speculation on the matter. Voices from the bar were raised loudly enough to penetrate along the corridor and into the room. Maria's eyes flashed their question at Crockett.

'Something's up,' he told her over his

shoulder and making for the cantiña itself with long, reaching strides.

As soon as he came through the rear door he saw the gaunt, distraught figure of Preacher Shalless, golden hair and beard awry and uncombed, black tie undone. He was waving his scarecrow-like arms, threatening at any moment to send shot-glasses on the bar crashing in a thousand fragments.

Maria, close behind Crockett, watched as Sheriff Frank Peck approached from the doors.

'What's all this, preacher?' he asked, breathing heavily with the exertion of one who carries a good deal of weight.

Seward Shalless wheeled at the sound of his voice. 'It's Lucy, Sheriff!' he exclaimed in his thin, cracked voice. 'She's missing! She can't—'

'Wait a minute, preacher,' Frank said. 'Hold yore hosses. What's all this about Lucy missin'? When did she leave town? Where did she go? Let's get the facts straight as we go along!'

Crockett, listening at the bar with Maria at his side, could not but help admire the way Frank handled the distraught fanatic. Peck was soon able to recapitulate the preacher's disjointed account in a way which made for clear understanding.

'Now then, Seward,' he said. 'Lucy left

town on a rested horse early this morning, aimin' to take out for the Mex villages in Eagle Tails valley. All right. You figger she should 'a' bin back long ago. But, heck, it's only a little after six o'clock now! Supposin' we wait a little while–'

'Lucy's come to some harm in this wicked land!' Shalless interrupted. 'I know it–' he broke off abruptly as he caught sight of Crockett at the door. 'You, sir! You, Mr. Crockett! You will help find my daughter! Harm has befallen her–'

Crockett said, cutting into the preacher's tirade, 'We can't do anything, tonight, Shalless. No one can pick up a trail and follow it in the dark. Like the sheriff says, we'd best wait until morning–'

'But you will help, Mr. Crockett? You will trail out with a posse, and you, Miss Cordoba – will you lend your Mexican mozo to help pick up any sign?'

Maria nodded, not knowing quite whether to smile or not. Crockett thought he would not remind the preacher that only a few days ago he strictly forbade any kind of communication or meeting between Lucy and himself.

Peck said, 'I'll get a posse together, Seward, and set out at first light. You take it easy now. I don't suppose Miss Lucy's come to any harm at all! Why, most likely her hoss has broke a leg. Maybe she's havin' to stay

181

overnight in the village!'

Shalless shook his head vacantly, muttering to himself. Suddenly, without any warning, as though realizing that he were in a sinful place, he wheeled sharply and shouldered his way through the batwing doors, leaving a silently speculative room behind him.

Though many were inclined to laugh at the fanaticism and brimstone methods of Preacher Shalless, all, without exception, acknowledged the possible dangers for Lucy, if indeed she had been out riding this wild and hostile country since early morning.

'He ain't got no right to let a purty girl like Miz Lucy go gallivantin' about the country,' one man opined.

'Sure!' another replied. 'Reckon it's askin' fer trouble what with Mex bandidos and reports of 'Paches...'

Maria's face was dark with concern. 'I do not lik' thees, Pheel! Why you trail out to look for thees so stupid girl? Deed not bot' she and her father forbid you to go near her?'

Crockett grinned slowly. 'So you heard that, Maria? I guess there's nothing very private in the Hondo Bends of this world. Maybe you're right in a way,' he went on seriously, 'but I'm out to get Vicente and when the right time comes, Skogee as well!

Maybe I can help myself as well as Shalless.'

Maria shrugged and turned away. Crockett could see anger in the tilt of her head and the squareness of her shoulders and wondered at this...

Just before the sun rose, Frank Peck's posse assembled outside the sheriff's office. There were about twenty townsmen, including both Crockett and Web Skogee, both of whom ostentatiously made a point of ignoring the other's presence.

It seemed to Crockett that the deputy looked a mite drawn and harassed. His brick-red face was not so red as usual and there was a shifting, anxious look in his normally bold eyes.

Peck, well aware of the possible dangers which might have befallen Lucy Shalless, saw to it that each member of his posse was well armed and well mounted. He was glad to have the services of Maria's mozo, Esteban, and pleased also that the army man, Crockett, was along. For now, Phil had revealed his identity, figuring that things were coming to a head and that to remain anonymous was no longer practical or desirable.

'It may be bandits or Injuns,' Peck told the assembled men gravely, 'but it may only be a false alarm. I guess we gotta be prepared for anythin'. You, Esteban and Lieutenant

Crockett, if you don't mind, I figure you'd best be in the lead.'

Skogee's malevolent gaze followed Crockett as he touched spurs to the gelding and gigged his mount to the front of the cavalcade, the little Esteban following close behind on one of Maria's finest horses.

'You all got water, guns an' shells and grub in yore pockets?' Frank Peck said. 'This might be a long chore. Let's go!'

With which brief speech the sheriff, suiting his action to the words, spurred his horse forward at a gentle trot, taking his place between Crockett and Esteban, the rest of the posse following at their heels.

CHAPTER 13

DEMAND FOR RANSOM

Web Skogee rode to the rear of the cavalcade answering the remarks of the rider who had paired off with him with monosyllabic grunts.

Once the man quit yapping, Skogee relapsed into a brooding silence, now and again lifting his glance and putting it ahead to where Crockett rode up in front. In his mind, Web Skogee was trying to sort things out, anxious and wondering as to the outcome of all this and cautious now in his play. Already he was figuratively poised for sudden flight, at the first real sign of danger. It looked as though his 'partnership' with Vicente were finished anyway. But there was the comforting thought of his cache of dollars back under the floorboards of his shack. Several thousand dollars which would see him along many a road if the need arose to quit the country.

He began to wonder what really *had* happened to Lucy, not because he was in the slightest bit genuinely concerned for her welfare, but because he had a sneaking and uncomfortable feeling that somehow her 'disappearance' tied in with his own problems.

All Hondo Bend had heard Crockett's brief report on the scattering of Vicente's band by the army – how the outlaw leader had been tricked – and Skogee ground his teeth at recollection of this, feeling evilly furious against Crockett as well as the sergeant who had feigned drunkenness.

But what now, he wondered. Crockett had admitted that Vicente himself had escaped, possibly with one or two companions. Skogee thought hard about this as the posse rode through the morning at a gentle trot.

The deputy knew this country pretty well, and now, in his mind he tried to imagine and follow the probable trails and direction Vicente would have taken in escaping from Hondo Bend. Once or twice, even, he swung round in his saddle, marking the bush-and-tree-fringed course of the Gila and the Hondo, now at their backs and dimmed by distance and the desert's dancing heat.

Skogee's black brows drew together with the very concentration of his thoughts. In the narrow corridor of his dark mind he figured he saw the faintest sliver of light. Vicente and perhaps Ramirez with him, would undoubtedly have made for the Eagle Tails, wherein was their permanent camp.

They would need food and supplies and fresh horses. That being so, they would have travelled northwards, perhaps north-west at first, to cross the Gila, before veering almost due west. Or, Web Skogee thought suddenly, if they had crossed the river farther south just above the Bend, they would logically arrive at Dame Valley, nestling between Dame Mountain and the Eagle Tails.

It came to Skogee then, that now and again Lucy travelled thus far, to the villages along the floor of the valley in her efforts to get 'converts' and school pupils. And there it was, suddenly, the whole picture clear in his mind, not certain sure but probably and feasible at least, according to his reasoning. Vicente had come across Lucy and had snatched her, thinking to hold her to ransom! It was just such a trick that the little outlaw would try – a trick probably born of desperation.

The more Skogee examined the idea, the more he was inclined to accept it as the truth; but just how all this would affect *him*, he was not quite sure.

He was beginning to feel that the time had come to withdraw quickly from this game. He still had his law job and county pay apart from his cache of dinero. It looked as though Vicente were all washed up, whether he had the girl or not. If the latter were true,

187

then there'd be such an uproar kicked up over the abduction of an Americano girl by a Mex bandit, that Maricopa and Yuma would soon be swarming with troops, lawmen and Governor's men!

In the middle of the forenoon, the sheriff halted the posse for a brief rest and to give the horses a blow. Men took sips from their canteens, some rolled smokes or cut chewing tobacco but none stepped out of saddles.

Within ten minutes or so, they were off again swinging round towards the distant Eagle Tails with Dame Mountain on their left flank.

At the head of the column Esteban called suddenly and sharply, pointing to the ground. Both Crockett and Peck dropped their gazes to the alkali and stone, trying to determine any tracks which might have caused Esteban to exclaim:

'Zere ees tracks of t'ree horses, Señor Crockett,' the little mozo said, 'ver' faint, but–'

'Could they have been made by Vicente and a couple of his men, Esteban?' Phil asked, realizing suddenly, even as Skogee had done, that Vicente, in all probability, would have ridden this way.

'Si, señor, but zen zey could be ze tracks of anyone. 'Ow would we know? Mebbe we ask an' find out at ze next village, huh?'

Frank Peck nodded. 'How far is it, Esteban? 'Bout five miles?'

The mozo nodded. 'Mebbe I go on a leetle ways an' watch thees tracks, huh?'

The sheriff turned enquiring eyes to Crockett.

Phil said: 'I reckon that's a good idea, Sheriff. Not so much chance of the posse mussing up what sign there is.'

Frank nodded and motioned Esteban forward. After that short pause and the near excitement caused by Esteban's discovery, the men moved forward again, muscles already stiffening as they sat their saddles and slitted their eyes against the dust and burning heat of the overhead sun.

Around noon, Frank signalled the tired men to rest for an hour and to eat some of their grub. Esteban having returned had found a near dried-up creek which yet contained enough trickling water for the horses to drink.

The actual place where the posse rested was only a few yards from where Vicente and Ramirez had met and abducted Lucy. This fact, or some of it, Esteban discovered after long and careful study of the faint tracks ahead.

He squatted on his bootheels in front of Peck and Crockett and the nearer of the posse members gathered around.

'Thees tracks, not t'ree, señores, but two

an' one, sabe?' He laughed at their obvious puzzlement. 'We figger t'ree riders mak' zees marks, huh? But only one rider she come first – Mees Lucy! Zen ze ot'airs, mebbe Vicente and un compadre overtak' her.' He pointed with his arm to the distant brush-choked cut-off, where he had spent a deal of time examining the ground.

'All zee tracks point along zee cut-off–'

'You figger they're headed towards Victente's hide-out up there?' Frank Peck asked, his arm pointed to the towering pine-clad slopes.

The mozo nodded and Crockett said: 'How old you figure those tracks, Esteban?'

The Mex was pretty sure without pondering unduly. 'Zey made yesterday, Señor Crockett, ees cairtain!'

Bexar of the mercantile spoke up then, and put their unvoiced thoughts into words.

'You split Vicente's gang up, day before yesterday at Hondo Bend. Give 'em a night an' a day to reach here, then they're gonna run smack into Lucy on her way to that there Mex village, or am I crazy?'

Crockett said: 'I don't figure you're crazy, Bexar. It sure looks like that's what probably happened. The point is where do we go from here?'

Frank Peck scratched his head and drew a hand down his sweaty, ponderous cheeks. But it was Esteban who answered.

'Esteban ride to Mex village; eet no tak' long time. Mebbe zey know somet'ing.' He scrambled to his feet and quickly adjusted cinch straps and latigo before jumping into leather.

'You wait 'ere for me to come back queeck, sabe?' Crockett nodded as the posse watched the indefatigable little mozo spur his horse along the trail in a lifting cloud of yellow dust...

The men found what sparse shade was available and thankfully stretched out to await Esteban's return. Skogee kept well in the background, while Frank Peck and Crockett walked over to the cut-off and made their own careful examination.

It was here that Phil took the opportunity of warning the sheriff about his deputy in a few terse sentences, telling him of the attempted ambush episode and also about the night he, Crockett, followed Skogee to the tarpaper shack and witnessed the sending off of the messenger, towards the Eagle Tails. At first Frank was angrily incredulous, but as Crockett quickly described all the things which pointed the finger of suspicion, Peck began to relax and examine the facts as they lay.

They were screened from the posse by the thick brush of the cut-off and well out of earshot.

191

'Why have you kept so all-fired quiet about this, Crockett, up 'till now?' Peck asked presently.

'It's pretty obvious, isn't it? I've got no proof, Sheriff, yet I *know* in my own mind that Skogee is an outside member of the gang, or some sort of partner perhaps!

'At first, he believed I was an undercover lawman, at least, that's the way I figure it. Apart from that there is a personal issue as well.'

Crockett told briefly of the attack on Lucy, not because he wanted to, but because now it was necessary for the sheriff to have every single correlated fact about his deputy.

'Could be,' Frank suggested, 'that Skogee tried to settle with you on account of the fight—'

'If it were just that alone,' Crockett interrupted, 'you could be right. But don't forget the incident of the man in the tarpaper shack. Whoever he was, he lit out in this direction with *two* saddlers and although it was dark, I saw enough to figure him as a Mex.

'Also, when I shot the member of Vicente's gang in El Cuchillo, Skogee nearly jumped out of his boots when he took a look at the dead Mex. He recognized him all right and what's more, Peck, *he knew him!*'

The sheriff pulled at his moustaches, his

face puckered up in thought.

'You got any ideas how we should play this, lieutenant?' he asked shortly.

'Things are boiling up to a climax,' Phil said slowly, 'and I don't see we can do more than give Web Skogee enough rope so he'll hang himself–'

Crockett's words were cut short by the sudden strike of boots on rock. Both men looked up from where they were hunkered down and gazed up into the black, beady eyes of Web Skogee!'

The silence ran on, sticky and wet, pulsating with feeling. Neither Peck nor Crockett could tell how much the deputy had heard of their conversation. Perhaps none at all, perhaps everything!

'Figger out anything from those tracks?' Skogee asked presently, breaking the long, building silence.

But they were spared the necessity of answering in the sudden rataplan of hooves pounding along the trail. The three men ran forward, emerging from the cut-off in time to witness Esteban slide from the saddle of his lathered horse. He held a piece of dirty paper in his hand which he waved excitedly as he looked around for Crockett and the sheriff.

'You got news, Esteban?' Peck shouted, coming forward at a run, for all his paunch.

'Goddam sure!' the mozo exclaimed,

handing the paper to Peck. 'Ees was geeven by a ragged peon een ze village. 'E say Vicente wants five t'ousand mejicano dollars for Señorita Lucy!'

'Here,' Peck said after studying the pencilled note. 'You're better at Spanish than me, Lieutenant. Read it, will you?'

Crockett took the paper, his eyes moving quickly over the half-illiterate scrawl. It abounded in spelling mistakes, but the gist of the message was unmistakable, just as Esteban had said.

Crockett nodded. 'Esteban's right. Vicente's got Lucy and wants five thousand Mex dollars prontito. Any attempt at a double cross and he's going to send us her ears first and other parts later–'

Peck's face darkened with fury. 'Hell!' he exploded, 'the damned dirty greaser–'

'That's not all, Frank,' Crockett put in. 'He wants the tall Americano, Crockett, to deliver the money by noon Wednesday and lay it at the foot of Mesa Rock. He says then he'll send the girl down. After that we both are to return to Hondo Bend, leaving the dinero at Mesa Rock for Vicente to pick up!'

Men were now gathered round talking excitedly, some contributing little more than cuss words and what they would do to all damned greasers if they had their way!

'Quiet!' Peck bellowed suddenly. 'We gotta figure this thing out. Hell! Noon Wednesday! That's tomorrow! If we play it like Vicente says, we get Lucy back but we get no chance of clappin' handcuffs on Tularez himself!'

Crockett said, after a moment, 'Esteban and I can remain here. We've got enough grub to last a couple more days. In any case you, Frank, can bring us some more when you return from town with the money–'

'How the heck–?' the sheriff began.

'It's your problem, Frank,' Crockett said evenly, 'but you've sure got to raise that dinero somehow and tote it back here by tomorrow morning.'

'You want the men to remain with you, Lieutenant?'

Phil shook his head. 'You-all high-tail back to Hondo Bend, pronto. You, Frank, and one other man only, return as fast as possible. It's no use our having a posse now.' Crockett went on, turning to the other men. 'This has got to be played like Vicente says – on the face of it, anyway, else Miss Shalless's life won't be worth a plugged nickel.'

'You know what yo're doin', Crockett?' Jud Little asked.

'Any man who wants the chore of leaving that dinero at Mesa Rock is sure welcome,' Crockett said coldly, eyeing Little until the saddler's gaze dropped.

Peck said: 'I figure the lieutenant knows

what he's doing and he's the one as started all this, an' got Vicente on the run. With the army's help, Crockett's already done what no one else could 'a' done – smashed Vicente's gang an' gotten the leader on the run.'

'Sure! Vicente's got the girl now an' for the moment there's nothin' we kin do 'cept get that dinero and hand it over!'

'Well, what are we waiting for?' a rider demanded, swinging into leather. 'Sooner we go, sooner she'll be back!'

The posse then made a concerted move towards their hobbled mounts. Some had saddles to throw on and cinch, but it took no more than a few minutes.

'Don't bring a crowd back with you, Frank,' Crockett murmured to the sheriff in the general confusion of men saddling and mounting. 'But if it's Skogee you bring back, then watch him all the time. I've got an idea how to play this thing.'

Crockett glanced towards the score or so of men. Some were aboard, others tightening cinches and bridling their animals.

'Sure, I'm going to place the money there, just like Vicente said and I'm waiting for Lucy to show up, too. We'll make tracks all right, but *I'm* coming back to watch that rock and grab whoever comes for the money!'

Frank nodded, but doubtfully. 'It's risky,

Lieutenant, but I see no other way.'

'There *is* no other way, Frank, and I'll be settling an old score before this chore is finished. Vicente, or one of his cut-throats killed my best friend on that first pay-wagon hold-up! Now Vicente's gang is down to a few men only and before long they too are going to be stretched out in the sun with the buzzards coming down...'

The sheriff looked keenly at Crockett. If ever there was retribution in a man's gaze it lay now in the lieutenant's hard eyes as they turned and lifted towards the massive mountains.

CHAPTER 14

A MATTER OF FIVE THOUSAND DOLLARS

It was late by the time the trail-weary posse hit town. Maria from the gallery could see no sign of Crockett in the light cast from the cantiña windows. Neither could she glimpse Esteban anywhere in that slow moving cavalcade of men as it moved into the light and pulled in to the hitch-rack. For a bitter, stabbing moment, she wondered whether Crockett and the mozo were both lying dead somewhere on the trail to the Eagle Tails.

It was only then that she noticed there was no Lucy Shalless accompanying Frank's posse and impulsively Maria ran across the board-walk and onto the dusty street, catching at the sheriff's bridle reins.

He looked down into that lovely anxious face, giving her the news straight away and showing her the pencilled ransom note which Vicente had written, holding it so the lamp's rays caught it.

She scarcely looked at that; relief flooded her face and shone in her eyes. Peck, with a rare flash of insight, grinned. 'You had it figgered Crockett was hurt, mebbe even killed?'

Maria's quick step backwards, the sudden wave of colour which surged into her cheeks, told the sheriff he had scored a bull's-eye.

He turned around in the saddle and thanked the posse-men, dismissing them. He watched as they gratefully hitched horses to the racks and started for saloons and cantiñas to wash the trail-dust from their parched throats.

'Web,' Peck said. 'Start in on getting that money from the bank–'

'Isn't it the preacher's pigeon?' Skogee demanded sourly.

'Maybe,' Peck said, 'but right now someone else has got to stand surety for that dinero, else the Governor's going to ask what we been doing to let an American woman get murdered by Mex outlaws!'

Skogee turned his horse towards the bank and Maria said suddenly and unexpectedly: 'Watch heem, Frank, 'e ees not so good, I am sure!'

Peck nodded. 'Crockett's told me,' he said simply. 'Now I suppose you wanta hear what happened an' why the lieutenant ain't back?'

She nodded. 'But hee ees all right, and Esteban also?'

'Both as fit as fleas,' Peck assured the girl, tying his horse to the rack and following her into El Cuchillo.

He leaned against the bar and thankfully downed the whisky which Maria herself poured, proclaiming that 'dreenks ees on the 'ouse!'

Frank smiled, feeling a little better. 'We gotta light out pronto, me an' Web an' tote five thousand dollars to Mesa Rock. Crockett's gotten himself the chore of leavin' the dinero for Tularez.'

'How?'

'Vicente himself stipulated it was to be left by the tall Americano, Crockett, and – hey! Come to think of it how in Hades did Vicente know his name less'n someone in Hondo Bend – yep! of course–'

'When you feenish talkin' een reedles an' to yourself, Shereef, pairhaps you would explain, si?'

'Cain't stop to explain now,' Frank said abruptly. 'Me an' Skogee gotta hit the trail prontito. You wanta help, Maria, pack some grub for Crockett and Esteban, huh?'

She nodded quickly, prepared immediately to do what she could.

'What time you feeger on leaving, Shereef?'

Peck glanced at the clock. The hands pointed to a little before eleven.

'Right away, Miz Maria. Soon as Web's

gotten the dinero an' you've packed the food. We ain't got any time to lose. It'll soon be Wednesday!'

Peck had wondered, in his own mind, about letting Skogee go down to the bank and see the official in charge on his own. It might be a temptation to the deputy to suddenly light out in the darkness and hit the trail for other places.

Moreover, there might be a deal of explaining necessary to the substitute manager to get the money at all. As it happened, Peck met his deputy midway between the bank and El Cuchillo. At least Skogee had saddled fresh horses for them but the absence of any gunny sack across the saddles, as well as Web's scowling face, told the sheriff that there was no dinero forthcoming.

'No dice, Frank,' Skogee growled. 'Thet bustard Hale, figures he ain't lettin' a dime go out of the bank apart to those holdin' accounts.'

Frank swore softly as he handed Skogee the packages of grub, indicating they should be shoved into saddle-bags.

'How's the canteens, Web?'

Skogee said 'Full of fresh water. What you going to do?'

Frank thought furiously. There was little time to roust out the town's leading citizens, Holt Caddo, Doc Treybor, and the like. By the time he had found enough of them and marched them all down to the bank several precious hours would be lost. Tularez was in a hurry and it would not do to keep him waiting just so long as he held the whip hand!

Maria stepped through the batwing doors, regarding the two shadowy figured lawmen in the street. She had been listening for their exit from the town and having failed to hear it had come out onto the street.

She crossed over now, walking quickly across the intervening ground.

'What ees the trouble, Shereef?'

'Hell, Miz Maria! How in heck are we gonna raise that ransom money in a matter of a few minutes? We ain't got time to waste! As it is, Web an' me'll haveta ride nearly all night–'

''Ow much dinero deed you say?'

Frank said, brightening: 'Five thousand Mex dollars, Miz Maria. Do you figure you could–?'

But she was gone in a whirl of skirts. Peck rolled a cigarette and waited with Skogee and the horses. Before the quirly was half finished, Jeff, the barman, came out toting a small, but weighty-looking sack.

He screwed up his eyes after the bright lights of the cantiña and, having accustomed them to the night, was able to pick out the figures of the two lawmen.

He grinned at Peck as he came towards them. 'Five thousand dollars, Sheriff, with Miss Cordoba's compliments.'

'Thanks, Jeff,' Peck murmured gratefully, 'and thanks to Miss Cordoba, too. I sure hope she can count good, Jeff, because there ain't no time to make a tally now!'

Jeff laughed and stepped back as the lawmen mounted, Peck with the sack across the saddle in front of him. 'Miss Cordoba's smart enough,' the barkeep assured them and Frank nodded and grinned, lifting his arm slightly as he put his horse to the night-enveloped trail...

Peck drew a vast sigh of relief as the first pale streaks of grey showed in the eastern sky. He had spent a hell of a night. Most of the time he had been riding, watching Skogee from the corner of his eye, ready to grab his gun should the deputy decide to make a sudden pounce for the money bag.

Why in hell hadn't he brought along Bexar and Little and a few others? At least they could be trusted and Skogee would never dare to make any dangerous play in the presence of these others.

As it was, Frank had to contrive to keep one eye on the trail, one eye on the money across his mount's withers and one eye on Skogee. All on top of the miles of riding that had been done in the last couple of days or so, it was one hell of a chore!

They had snatched a few hours' sleep before dawn. At least Skogee had! Was even now snoring peacefully while Peck knuckled his eyes to ease the pain and weight of his swollen lids.

He hadn't dared drop off, figuring that at any time Skogee might take it in his head to call it a day, shoot the sheriff and just quietly vamos into the night with the five thousand dollars!

Thus, when the eastern sky began to pale, Sheriff Frank Peck felt something of the heavy weight slip from his aching shoulders and tired mind. He cursed quietly for some few moments as he watched Web Skogee's brick-red face, peaceful in repose in the light from the miserable little fire which Peck had sanctioned.

The sheriff stretched himself now, still holding the carbine with which he had mounted guard explaining to Skogee the necessity for this.

Whether Web had seen through the excuse, whether or not he had thought about jumping Peck, the sheriff didn't know. That was partly what had irritated Frank so much – the fact of having to stay awake when in reality, it might not have been necessary.

During that long and uncomfortable night ride, with neither man talking overmuch, the subject of Skogee's thoughts had been entirely problematical as far as Frank was concerned. Any sudden though innocent move on the deputy's part had caused Peck to stiffen and half claw for his gun. It had gotten to the point when Peck figured Skogee was trying to get him rattled; deliberately making these sudden, quick moves in order to laugh at him, but quietly!

For his part, Skogee had already, long ago, considered the idea of killing Peck and making off with the ransom money, but had almost immediately rejected the idea. Not because of any feeling for Lucy Shalless or Frank Peck, but because there were other and bigger fish to fry, tomorrow or the next day!...

Skogee sat up and yawned, rolling out of his blankets with the lazy ease of a man who had slept well. Peck eyed him with ill-disguised disgust.

There was the same thin trickle of water here which they had discovered on the journey to town and now Peck quietly sluiced face and hands, his carbine beside him.

He gathered extra brush on the way back, and placed it atop the smouldering coals which he had kept going during the latter part of the night.

They breakfasted in silence as the sky lightened and became shot with blue, gold, saffron and madder.

In a little while they were in leather, heading along the trail which would lead them to Crockett and Esteban…

Esteban said, keening the wind, his face sharp and thin, 'Zey come, Señor Crockett, I t'ink!'

Phil rose from the blanket and saddle, stretched himself and moved to the small screened fire, pouring himself a cup of coffee.

'You sure it's the sheriff, Esteban?'

The little Mex shrugged and grinned. 'Quien sabe? *Someone* ees coming. Pairhaps I better go an' mak' goddam sure!'

Crockett nodded, watched the mozo saddle up quickly and point his horse to the trail.

He was beginning to feel tight inside, as he always did before action. He was not kidding himself about this chore. It was going to be dangerous. Bullets would fly and people would be killed. Of that, Crockett was certain, because inasmuch as *he* was going to try a double-cross on Vicente, it was as obvious as Mesa Rock itself, that the bandit chief would try the same thing. Such men, Crockett knew, scarcely ever kept their word. Kidnapping was a federal rap and even though Arizona was a territory and not a state, the snatching of an American girl was likely to cause quite a ruckus. Angry senators would demand action from the Governor at Prescott once the news leaked out and the Governor, in turn, would jump on the necks of all lawmen in Yuma and Maricopa Counties, particularly the sheriff and his deputy in Hondo Bend.

Vicente was no fool, and he would have this all figured out. He would know that by returning the girl, he was not going to give himself a clean bill of health as far as the law was concerned. Whatever he thought about such things as an amnesty, and perhaps this was where Tularez was not so clever, the fact remained that there were enough charges against him for murder and robbery to string him up a dozen times.

If Vicente realized this, which was very probable, Crockett thought, then he might well try to grab the money *and keep the girl as well!*

It was probable, too, that if Vicente succeeded in this he would make his final break with Yuma or Maricopa counties; maybe even cross the Colorado into California, free to restart his operations and build up his depleted band again.

All that being so, Crockett knew there would be lead flying around Mesa Rock pretty soon and in his present restless mood, the sooner the better!

He knew it was risky having Skogee along, though maybe Frank would decide to leave him back in town. But Crockett didn't think so. He had intimated to the sheriff that he had some sort of plan, a pretty vague one, however, which included Web Skogee. Crockett's idea was that if Vicente and his men saw the deputy with the sheriff and himself they might decide to settle with him, figuring that Skogee now stood four-square with the law.

There was something else, too, which Phil Crockett had in mind, and was not forgetting; that was the dinero which Vicente must have cached somewhere in or around his camp. But that would be the last chore of all. Before the money could be recovered or even looked for, Tularez himself and the remains of his gang would have to be settled with!

Phil rolled and lit a cigarette, glancing down the rough trail and seeing the three riders approaching, at some distance.

He squinted his eyes against the lifting sun, presently identifying Esteban in the lead with Peck and Skogee following. A half-hour or so later, the three rode into camp and the two lawmen climbed wearily from leather.

Frank took down the money sack and handed it to Crockett.

'Here's the dinero, Lieutenant, but you'd better count it. How long's it going to take you to reach Mesa Rock?'

Phil looked at Esteban and the little Mex said, 'No more zan an hour, Shereef, t'rough ze foot'ills.' He raised his eyes to the sun and added, 'We 'ave t'ree hours – plenty goddam time!'

Crockett was already riffling through the bills and stacking the gold pieces into fives and the silver dollars into twenties. He looked up as Peck helped himself to a cup of coffee at the fire.

'How come the bank didn't make this easier to tote by giving you all bills, Frank?'

Peck sank down onto a blanket with a vast sigh of relief. His gaze shuttled across to where his deputy was unsaddling both horses and feeding them a little of the grain which Web had brought along.

'The bank wouldn't play ball, Lieutenant,' Peck said, returning his gaze to Crockett. 'Guess I mighta known they'd want some pretty heavy authority for advancing five thousand without surety.'

'Then, how–?'

Frank smiled then and said inconsequentially, 'You know, Crockett, I'm beginning to think that Hondo Bend wouldn't be much of a place without Maria Cordoba!'

Crockett's thick brows came up. He stopped counting the money for a moment, surprise momentarily holding his hands and brain still.

'You mean *Maria* dug up this money, Sheriff?'

Peck nodded. 'Wasn't much time to go rousting out the town's leading citizens. By the time we'd 'a' done that and explained everything, even if they was willing, we might not 'a' made it here on time!'

Phil nodded and returned to the task of counting. It didn't take long and shortly he pulled open the sack and shoved the money back – bills, silver and gold pieces all together.

'Five thousand it is, Frank, thanks to Maria Cordoba! Now we can get started.'

'What you want us to do?' Peck asked. 'This is yore party, Lieutenant, so just say your piece and we'll back your play all the way!'

'You've got to watch Skogee,' Phil said, lowering his voice a little and glancing in the deputy's direction. 'I can't figure out ahead what his play is going to be, but I'd say the man being a coyote, he'll do just what a coyote would.'

'You mean he'll hold back until the shooting's over and then try and grab himself a handful of the spoils?'

Crockett nodded. 'I'm also not sure what the spoils will be,' he said grimly. 'Maybe a blonde girl, maybe a cache of gold, maybe nothing but hot lead.'

'My gun's siding you, Crockett,' Frank

said, climbing to his feet, 'and I ain't considered a bad shot. Seems like my job'll be to cover you an' Esteban and watch Skogee at the same time?'

'A sizeable chore, Frank, big enough to keep most men busy!'

'Not too big,' Peck said soberly and softly added, 'I hope!'

CHAPTER 15

SLAUGHTER AT MESA ROCK

For a little over a half-hour, Esteban rode stirrup to stirrup with Crockett, then, at a sign from the other, the mozo neck-reined his horse from the narrow cut-off and plunged into a wilderness of rocky canyons and brush- and thicket-choked trails, immediately losing himself from view.

Crockett felt very much alone now. The sun was climbing to its meridian and was turning the land oven-hot. A hell of a time to pick, Crockett thought, wiping sweat from his face. High Noon! A hell of a time and a hell of a place! But then, Vicente had been giving the orders. He knew the stupid importance that the gringos attached to their womenfolk and he would be pretty certain that the dinero would be laid on the barrel – or at the foot of Mesa Rock – at the time and date stipulated. Crockett could see the great colour-slashed sentinel now as a bend in the rough track brought it into full view and clear focus. He glanced anxiously at the sun but realized it wanted a full half-hour to noon.

Crockett rode on slowly in this heat-scarred land. Nothing moved in the absolute stillness as far as he could see and no sound broke the vast silence save for the gelding's iron shoes as they struck rock; the faint yet reaching squeak of leather and jingle of bridle chains.

Crockett was in a world of his own, or so it seemed, yet he remembered with thankfulness that somewhere behind, amongst those oven-hot rocks and scrub, Frank Peck and Skogee were watching and somewhere off to one side the little mozo had his black eyes glued to Crockett's slow moving figure. Yet, even now, when this land seemed more barren and empty than ever before, the lieutenant felt the strike of eyes on him, like a physical thing, almost, as he did when riding on a scouting patrol into the Apache hills.

The rock was near now, a scant quarter-mile away, rising straight up from the jumble of boulders and eroded stone at its base.

Crockett saw the narrow trail which he had taken the last time he was here, sweeping round the base of the mesa and ribboning upwards to lose itself amongst the jagged shapes higher up. Recollection of that last time caused the skin to tighten on his face. Involuntarily he wiped the sweat from his face with the neckerchief and took a fresh grip on the sack across the saddle.

His gaze slid over the nearby rocks, upwards and sideways, yet never so much as a flash of a brown face or chihuahua hat did it intercept.

He slid from leather and toted the sack the last few feet, feeling the nerves on his neck and back tingle as he leaned forward and dropped the money in a conspicuous spot near the thin, ribbon-like trail.

He stepped back, pausing only to rub his wet hands down his denim pants and slowly, watchfully, climbed back into leather. He heard the faintest trickle of sand then, as an unseen horse kicked a loose stone. A man's voice, muted and low, cursed quietly in Spanish. Crockett's right hand rested on his thigh; the Colt was a bare inch behind his wrist, as he watched the trail and heard the sharp clatter of hooves rise suddenly into the breathless air.

They came down at a fair lick, their ponies sure-footed as mountain goats. There were three of them, all Mexicans, and Crockett knew then, quite certainly, that Vicente had no intention of exchanging the girl for the money. *He was going to have both of them!*

Vicente, Crockett felt sure, was the fat, swaggering figure atop the gaily caparisoned black horse. All three Mexes were masked and Phil realized suddenly that none of Vicente's band had ever been identified.

He knew as he sat there in the saddle that his life was hanging on the slenderest of spider-web threads, but the imminence of violent explosive action tempered Crockett's nerves to a cool, steely alertness. Here was the prelude to gun-play and fast thinking, where a man either emerged triumphantly or went down to taste for the last time the bitter dregs of defeat and – death!

Black eyes glittered above silk masks in the strong shadows cast from the wide, sugar-loaf hats and glances slid from this tall man in the saddle to the sack of money lying against the burning heat of the rocks.

Crockett's nerves tightened an infinitesimal fraction as the fat one lifted his right hand and pulled down his mask. Crockett was alert for the first sign of trouble, taking this movement as a possible signal. Even whilst his glance remained on the mounted trio he contrived to glimpse any movement or threatening danger on the path and amongst the rocks behind them. But nothing moved and the fat ugly little bandit chief smiled wickedly as his glance came back from the sack and settled on Crockett's face.

'Ees good you breeng thees dinero, señor,' he grinned, his jowls wobbling to the movement of his lips. 'You quite sure, Señor Crockett, eet ees five t'ousand like I say?'

Crockett as still as a statue and never

taking his eyes from the bunched riders said, 'There's five thousand all right, Vicente, I counted it myself. Now, what about the Americano girl? We've kept our side of the bargain!'

'Ah, yes!' Tularez smiled and rolled his eyes from side to side. 'You know I am Vicente, si? But zees knowledge do you no good, señor–' Even as he spoke, Vicente's glance flickered over the man on his left. It came so suddenly, in the middle of his talking that as prepared as he was, Phil nearly came unstuck. The Mex's hand was up and moving back from his neck, sunlight glinting on the wide-bladed throwing knife, almost before Crockett's had reached back for his gun.

Somehow or another, the lieutenant made an amazingly fast, clean draw. The hammer was back before the barrel had cleared leather; the gun roared and the bullet took the Mex in the chest before ever the knife left his hand. The force of the .45 slug knocked him sideways in the saddle, the knife clattering to the ground and already Crockett's gun was swinging round to draw a bead on Vicente, the most dangerous and reptilian of the trio.

Phil sensed in those tense death-laden moments, that Tularez had no intention of letting him get away. He had betrayed that intention by pulling down the mask and revealing his face. Perhaps that brash action had warned Crockett and given him the edge on the double-dealing outlaw.

But the scene suddenly changed as Crockett threw down on Vicente and hammered a too-fast shot at the little renegade, even while the remaining Mex was levering a shell into the breech of his drawn carbine.

The crack of a Winchester sounded off somewhere to Crockett's rear and for a fraction of time, his gun wavered as the gelding under him moved in alarm at the carbine's sharp explosion.

Crockett's bullet whined past Vicente's head and the outlaw's face turned greasy and yellow as death whispered in his ear. Vicente's own mount reared but somehow, either by sheer luck or else expert marksmanship, his gun arced down at Crockett simultaneously belching flame and hot lead.

Crockett reeled as the bullet struck home. He felt himself falling, yet some instinct caused him to kick his feet free and hold tight to the six-gun in his hand as he fought to retain his reeling senses.

He hit the ground hard and the solid impact against rock and stone seemed to clear his mind for a few moments of the cobwebby mists that threatened to envelop his hammering brain.

He was dimly aware of a sudden upsurge

of firing; carbines joining in with six-guns and – Crockett shook his head like a dog throwing off water – *he heard the unmistakable crash of a heavy calibre Sharp's rifle...*

Immediately after Jeff had handed the sack of money to the sheriff, he returned to the bar to find Maria standing there, one arm resting lightly on the polished red-wood top.

There were few customers at this late hour and what men there were, drank or played at the tables, except for a few who danced with percentage girls to the three-piece band.

Maria said, 'Tell Gonzales to take over for a leetle while, Jeff, and follow me.'

Jeff nodded and, having indicated to the houseman to look after the bar, followed Maria through into the rear parlour.

'I do not lik' thees, Jeff,' she said as soon as the man had closed the door. 'Thees business of ransom money an' for Crockett to tak' eet heemself. Eet ees a trap! I know eet, I feel eet here!' She touched her heart with a tightly clenched fist.

'Vicente weel not allow the Señor Crockett to return, nor weel he geeve up Lucy.'

'You figure he wants the girl *and* the dinero, ma'am?' Jeff asked, rolling and lighting a quirly. 'Surely he wouldn't wanta be hog-tied with the girl once he gets his hooks on the dinero?'

'I theenk, yes,' Maria replied soberly. 'I know hees breed. 'E weel not be content to concede anytheeng! Thees men are born to double-cross, Jeff, and Crockett ees een great danger.'

'You care about that, ma'am?' Jeff said and then, looking at her closely added, 'I see you do. Heck! Why the hell should he take the rap for the Shalless girl anyway? What's that old turkey-buzzard doing about it?'

'Not'ing, I fear,' Maria said angrily, 'but *I* am doing somet'ing, prontito!

'Señor Pete 'ad to go, like Vicente said. Also the lootenant has a job to do heemself. The army pay-roll, remember?'

'Sure,' Jeff nodded, 'but what can we do? How can we help Crockett? I guess maybe I might ride to Dame Valley myself an' side him. I can use a gun–'

Maria shook her head. 'Eet would be too late, Jeff, ef you went. I know all the trails and cut-offs. Esteban 'as shown me. I worry over Esteban as well. No, Jeff. You stay 'ere, I weel go now, just as soon as you saddle me a hoss, pronto.'

'I don't like it, ma'am,' Jeff said frowning. 'This country ain't no place for a woman to go sashayin' about even in daytime let alone at night.'

'You get thees hoss saddled, Jeff,' Maria said quietly. 'I helped the Señor Crockett before, remember? Maybe I can again. Also

219

I am scared of Web Skogee. I do not trust heem. Now, 'urry, Jeff, while I go and get ready; there ees not so much time!'

Maria decided that her usual long and voluminous dresses or skirts would not be very practical on such a mission as this.

Quickly she donned whipcord trousers and Justin boots and shrugged into an old denim jumper, finally crowning her black hair with a wide-brimmed, low-crowned stetson.

She did not waste time on unessential things and within ten minutes she was at the barns in back of El Cuchillo.

By the lantern's light, Jeff handed her a leather poke of shells and indicated the Sharp's rifle in the saddle scabbard.

She saw at once that Jeff had picked the best animal for the job. An ugly, hammer-headed buckskin with long legs and a deep chest.

Rather awkwardly, Jeff wiped a hand on his apron front and held it out to Maria in an embarrassed silence.

The girl smiled and returned his hand-clasp, springing into the saddle and pointing the buckskin out of the barn and towards the patio gate.

'Good luck, ma'am,' Jeff said huskily as the small dark figure spurred the horse out onto the street and galloped away into the night.

Once clear of town, Maria oriented herself

by the stars and by insignificant yet well-known landmarks. Wherever possible she kept the buckskin to an easy lope, occasionally pulling it in to a walk where the trail became more rocky and dangerous.

She knew that she had plenty of time. The lawmen could not be more than two hours ahead and would probably rest for an hour or two before dawn. Nevertheless, they all had a long ride to make and once the sun was up the going would be tough in the heat of the desert.

She had till noon tomorrow to fetch up at Mesa Rock and with this thought in mind, chose the shelter of a rocky bluff around midnight to rest both herself and the buckskin gelding.

She munched on the cold provisions which Jeff had placed in the saddle-bags and shortly, fed the buckskin a little grain from the sack tied to the saddle cantle.

Maria was determined not to go to sleep this time, and having eaten and seen to the horse, paced slowly up and down until she figured by the westering moon, two hours had gone by.

She tightened cinches on the double rigged saddle and slipped the bit back into the animal's mouth. She was glad to be in the saddle again, though the flat country was lonely and eerie in the soft star and moonlight.

Once a coyote howled from a nearby ridge, startling both horse and rider and, way off, on some distant rocky ridge a catamount gave its frightening scream-like roar.

Maria was content to ride slowly now. She was approaching the stony trail which ribboned out from the bluffs and low buttes of the desert towards the distant mountains.

Twice she rested the horse and judged her position carefully. It was dark now, but in a little while the eastern sky would lighten to herald a new day. There was still some distance to go and Maria determined to travel as much of it as possible under cover of darkness. Once she thought she saw the winking light of a distant camp fire and wondered whether it were made by the sheriff and his deputy. It could be, or it could be an outlaw's night fire or even the brief camping place of some Apaches. She shivered slightly against the pre-dawn wind and lifted the reins, the game buckskin responding eagerly in spite of the miles it had covered...

It was Maria's thorough training in reading sign which now saved her from running smack into the sheriff and his deputy.

Previously what sign there had been, was scuffed and dust-blown, difficult even for a Mex tracker or an Apache to read.

Nevertheless the girl knew more or less

what to look for and the general direction in which any fresh tracks would be pointing. Esteban was paired with Crockett and, last night, Frank Peck and Web Skogee had taken out towards Crockett's camp with the money.

Thus, any fresh tracks ought to show up as two sets for the lawmen and then, later, in all probability four distinct sets, unless – and here Maria drew rein to study the country ahead – unless Crockett and Esteban separated from the lawmen...

Maria stepped from leather, crouching down over the hard surface of the ground, with its superimposed dusting of alkali and mica particles.

She studied the tracks for a long while, unmindful of the sun's increasing heat as it climbed to its zenith.

This was the entrance to the dry, arid valley between Dame Mountain and the Eagle Tails and suddenly, Maria's gaze, probing ahead, saw the spot which undoubtedly had marked Crockett's camp. The sign was not obvious but yet apparent to this girl, whose eyes and brain had been lessoned by the astute Esteban.

Careful that her actions were not conspicuous, Maria remounted the buckskin and spurred it towards the now deserted 'camp.' Anxiously her gaze traversed the ground and then lifted to the sun. She had

had plenty of time in hand last night, but a good deal of that leeway had been lost by the slow travelling necessary to cover this stretch of country unobserved, in daylight.

She had carefully guarded against raising any kind of dust cloud, however small, and had hugged the low buttes and rocks, using every inch of cover to screen her from any prying eyes in the foothills. Thus, she had somewhat miscalculated, and it was with a quite audible cry of triumph that she spied the two sets of tracks quartering to the brush-choked cut-off.

Now, in this narrow tangled trail, circumnavigating the base of the Eagle Tails and leading, as she sensed, directly to Mesa Rock, she could make up some of her lost time.

Even then, she heard the crack of a gun and the thin scream of a bullet before she was able to round the piled up rocks at the foot of the Mesa itself.

She urged the buckskin to the fullest extent, risking a throw and a possible broken leg in her fierce resolve to get to the scene of action quickly.

At the base of the Mesa, she swung out of leather, drawing the Sharp's rifle with her as she ground-tied the buckskin, moving swiftly but carefully around the big rock.

She saw Crockett then, similarly placed as he had been before. But this time there were *three* Mex riders and there was no humour in this repetition of previous events and no mirth in the girl's dark eyes as she heard a carbine join in, saw Vicente level his gun and shoot and saw, with a sickening foreboding, Crockett's body slide from leather.

He was on the ground, the six-gun still in his hand, when the buffalo gun roared out its crashing defiance, sending waves of noisy echo ricocheting around and off the rocks.

But frighteningly close and shocking was the sudden sight of Web Skogee, a smoking carbine in his hand and the body of Frank Peck sprawled some fifty yards away, both of them in a shallow basin of rock and just about screened from Vicente's view.

In that split-second of time in which Maria's decision had to be made almost at the same moment as witnessing the dual action, she swung the rifle round so that the sights were aligned not on Web Skogee but on Vicente's fat body.

The heavy calibre slug smashed into his breastbone, knocking him backwards from the saddle to fall amidst the cluster of rocks. He twitched once and then lay quite still, his sightless eyes gazing up into the brassy sky, blood pumping from his smashed body.

Maria dragged her gaze away, re-cocking the rifle as she traversed the barrel back to Skogee. But the second Mex had, by now, levered a shell into the carbine's breech and had essayed a shot at the half-conscious Americano on the ground. Providentially, Pedro was one of many such Mex bandidos who were careless about their guns, particularly when it came to cleaning them. Whatever the reason, the fact remained that the hammer jammed in spite of every effort to pull the trigger.

But another rifle echoed out amongst the rocks and from the corner of her eyes, Maria thankfully glimpsed the small, lithe figure of Esteban. In the tense and dramatic action of the past few minutes – or was it hours? – she had entirely forgotten the existence of the little mozo or where he was at. Gunsmoke filled the girl's nostrils and heat beat down from the sky and over all was the reek of drifting powder fumes and high above the Eagle Tails, black specks were already hovering in the sky!

But though Esteban had arrived in time to deal with Pedro and thanks to the jammed gun had killed him, that brief distraction caused by the mozo's timely action had been sufficient to retard Maria's finger on the trigger.

Skogee, feet planted well apart, was now perched on the rock wall from where he could view the entire scene. He thought fast and aimed well, choosing the girl because, firstly she was the nearer of his enemies and secondly, he feared that buffalo gun more than he did Esteban's much lighter .30-.30 carbine!

Maria felt the jarring shock of the bullet as it ripped through her and then almost immediately, a tidal wave of pain enveloped and choked her, so that she fell forward onto the rocks, not even feeling the upthrown heat of the stones.

CHAPTER 16

IN THE SHADOW OF THE ROCK

Esteban was bitterly torn between the desire to smash the deputy or run to the aid of Maria Cordoba.

Sweat ran down the little mozo's leathery face; the sweat of fury and savage purpose. His glance went down to the still figure in trousers and boots which he had no difficulty in identifying as his beloved mistress.

He swung the carbine wildly and fired, once, twice and then in a furious rage, emptied the magazine at the fast disappearing Web Skogee.

But the shots had been hurried and passion had caused Esteban's carbine barrel to waver. Meanwhile, Skogee had used the few minutes' grace in which to put more distance between himself and the avenging mozo.

Skogee was figuring that things had shaped up pretty well and he was not going to crowd his luck by offering himself as a target to the wily Esteban!

With Vicente and the rest of his band dead, with Maria and Crockett either killed or badly wounded, the way would be open now for the deputy not only to collect the ransom money which still lay unclaimed at the foot of Mesa Rock, but to go after the fortune in gold and silver which he knew Vicente must have cached somewhere around his hide-out, farther up into the mountains.

But Dame Fortune, shifting sides with the perverseness and inconstancy, directed the last erratically fired bullet from Esteban's carbine against Skogee's retreating figure even as he gained the shelter of thick brush and low bluffs where both the lawmen's horses were ground-anchored.

Skogee half-fell, half-stumbled out of sight and range of the mozo's gun, Esteban remaining ignorant of the fact that he had even winged the lawman.

He scrambled down the rocks now, towards the girl as Crockett managed to push himself to an upright position, six-gun still gripped tightly in his right hand.

Both men heard the sudden, sharp clatter of hoofs on rocks and Crockett, wiping sweat and dirt from his eyes, thumbed back the hammer of his gun with a gigantic effort, putting his gaze towards the steep grade on which a rider appeared with startling abruptness.

Esteban was feverishly feeding fresh shells into the Winchester's breech and froze suddenly as he gazed wide-eyed at the dishevelled figure of Lucy Shalless astride a bare-back horse and holding a six-gun in her hand.

Crockett eased back the hammer of his gun and then, belatedly turned his head to survey the scene behind him. He saw Esteban bending beside a dark-clad figure sprawled away behind him and to his left. He saw no sign of Frank Peck or Skogee and returned his glance to where Lucy, white with fright, swerved her mount clear of the sprawled figures of the dead bandidos.

In a moment or two, despite her fright, Lucy Shalless had taken in the immediate situation. Indeed here at the scene of battle was a story which revealed itself graphically enough in the grim, bloody tableau of dead and wounded men.

Crockett was fumbling at the sticky-wet flesh-wound in his thigh, when Lucy put her mount forward with a sudden squaring of her chin and a light of determination in her eyes.

She half slid from her mount's slippery back and knelt down beside Crockett, the fear in her suddenly evaporating in the face of the man's urgent need.

She wasted no time in idle questions but bent to the task of bathing Crockett's leg. Having cut the trousers away around the wound and fetched the canteen from the gelding's saddle, she cleansed the wound as adequately as possible, binding it tightly with strips torn from her petticoats.

She put the canteen to Crockett's dry lips and allowed him to gulp down a little of the precious, luke-warm liquid.

He grunted and pushed the water-bottle away, lifting his glance to her white, dust-smeared face.

'You all right, Lucy?' he croaked, essaying a feeble grin through the mask of dirt and sweat.

She nodded quickly. 'I managed to get free soon after they all left the camp. There were only the four of them left, Vicente, Pedro, Arispe and Ramirez. I managed to catch a horse from the cavvy but there was no saddle. Arispe was there. He – he tried to stop me. I shot him.' She choked on the words as she indicated the big Colt lying on the ground.

'I brought it along – was prepared to use it too,' she said, taking a deep breath, 'but I think there is no need to worry now. There are no bandidos left! How does your leg feel? It is a bad hole but the bullet has gone clean through.'

Crockett said, 'I guess I'm okay, Lucy, thanks. Climb up onto that rock and have a look around. Peck and Skogee should be nearby.'

She made for the rock and quickly

ascended to the top. She put her gaze over the immediate country, spotting the distant figure of the sheriff, sprawled face downwards. She knew it was Peck by the shape of him and the striped trousers he invariably wore and red-backed vest.

'It's Peck,' Lucy said returning from the rock, 'and it looks as though he may be dead. At least he's been shot. I must go down and see what I can do–'

'Who else is here?' Crockett asked. 'I can't see who it is Esteban is attending.'

Lucy stood up and called to the mozo in Spanish.

'Eet ees Señorita Cordoba,' he replied in a high, cracked voice, 'she ees badly wounded!'

'Hell!' Crokett said between his teeth. 'See what you can do to help Esteban, Lucy, before you go down to Frank.'

'You will be all right if I leave you a little while?' the blonde girl asked anxiously.

'Sure,' he nodded, 'and take the rest of that water with you, Lucy.'

The gelding had not strayed above thirty yards or so and was pulling at the foliage of a straggling mesquite shrub.

Crockett whistled and the animal turned and whinnied, eyeing its master curiously as he struggled to climb to his feet.

Blood pounded in Phil's head as he stood swaying a little, favouring his left, tightly bandaged leg. He called to the gelding again and the animal now came forward careful to keep its forelegs free of the trailing reins.

Phil patted the glossy neck and fished into the nearest saddle-pocket, withdrawing a pint bottle of whisky. He uncorked the bottle and tilted it to his mouth, feeling a sudden upsurge of renewed strength as the raw spirit coursed through him.

Half-leaning against the gelding, he contrived to clean the dust and dirt from his gun and refill the empty chambers, his sober glance now and again straying to where Esteban had pulled Maria into a small patch of shade.

The little mozo came forward now and almost immediately Lucy appeared from the rock basin, wherein Peck lay, bloody and unconscious.

The three of them, in the lengthening shadow of Mesa Rock, held a brief council.

'Peck is not dead, Mr Crockett,' Lucy gasped, breathing hard after her exertions, 'but he is badly hurt. He needs a doctor, pronto, and so does Miss Cordoba!'

Crockett nodded. 'You must ride back to town as fast as you can, Esteban. Take yours and Maria's horse. Miss Shalless and I will wait here for you to return with a medico and a spring-wagon.'

'Si, Señor Crockett. I weel ride lik' the weend. We weel be back before dawn weet' the Americano, Doctor Treybor. But what 'as happened to thees deputy, Skogee? I keel heem goddam queeck when–'

'He's gotten away,' Lucy interrupted quickly, 'and by the look of things has taken Frank Peck's horse as well. I found where they had tied them, but there was no sign of Web. Oh, Mr. Crockett,' Lucy exclaimed miserably, 'hasn't there been enough killing and fighting already, and why is Esteban talking of – of killing the deputy?'

Crockett told Lucy the story in a few brief sentences. She listened wide-eyed with horror. 'Will it make your fellow-officer come back? Will it take the bullet from Maria Cordoba's body, this killing of yet another man?' she asked in a tight voice.

'There's no time to argue the ethics of the thing,' Crockett said harshly, not bothering to remind the girl that she had killed a bandit in order to live herself. 'Get going, Esteban, and don't worry about Skogee. I've got one last chore to do myself and I'm going to follow that double-crossing murderer, if needs be, to the end of the trail...'

Crockett lay belly down amongst a solid-packed scattering of rocks, a bare fifty yards from Mesa Rock itself. And as the sun climbed higher and poured down its heat, the lieutenant sweated and reflected on whether he had gauged Skogee correctly in betting that he would return here as soon as the coast was clear.

The sack of money, the five thousand dollars ransom money, still lay at the foot of the gigantic rock, a tempting bait in the morning sunshine.

But would it prove a strong enough bait to draw Web Skogee back from whatever trail he had taken yesterday?

Crockett thought back, too, on the happenings of last night. He and Lucy had waited together in an almost silent vigil, watching the unconscious Maria and the moaning, delirious sheriff, whom Esteban had brought out from the rock basin across the saddle of his own horse before leaving for Hondo Band.

Once or twice Lucy had attempted conversation, but Crockett's mind was on the lovely Spanish girl who again had risked her life, this time riding dangerously near death, in her effort to save him from harm.

Phil had counted off the slow moving hours, figuring the time it would take the mozo to reach Hondo Bend, even with a spare fresh horse. Esteban was a fine rider and the urgency of Maria's condition would spur him on to the maximum effort. But then, another hour would have to be allowed for him to roust out the doctor and Clay Bellenger and procure fresh horses and a wagon...

But Esteban had returned ahead of the spring-wagon before dawn, and Clay Bellenger, for all that Maria held those wanted bills over him, had driven his horse furiously through the night as though all hell were at his heels.

When the doctor had finally arrived, dawn was paling the eastern sky and the dust of hard and fierce riding was still hung on the desert air.

Doc Treybor, a small capable medico, had examined Maria at the first light of day and had cleansed and disinfected the wound in her side. He could not then attempt the operation of removing the bullet but contented himself with preparing the blanket and straw pallets which Clay had placed in the bed of the wagon.

Treybor had also tended to the sheriff and had given the delirious lawman a draught of something to ease the pain and render him completely unconscious.

There had been arguments after that about Crockett's remaining behind. Treybor had mildly remarked that the lieutenant's leg needed rest and attention. But finally, in the full light of day, they had driven away, leaving the army man bitterly resolved to play his hunch that Skogee would not only be back for the money sack but would probably continue on to Vicente's now deserted camp and search for further spoils...

Crockett's gelding was hidden away safely under an overhang of rocks nearby, but Phil knew there was an even chance that Skogee had been watching, from some vantage point, and had seen the wagon take out for Hondo Bend. Whether or not he would have been able to determine from a distance who had ridden back in the wagon and how many, even, was another matter. But although the forenoon crawled away and the sun beat down from overhead, the land remained quiet and seemingly uninhabited save the three dead Mexicans over which the buzzards circled lower and lower...

Crockett tried to concentrate on his vigil while his mind went back over the actions of the men and women in Hondo Bend. Peck, Skogee, Shalless and the others, and then – Lucy herself and Maria.

Lucy, on her own admission, had killed a man. She had committed the 'crime' for which both she and her father had condemned Crockett. He grinned to himself, shifting his sweaty grip on the carbine stock and pulling his hat well down over his eyes against the intense glare of the sun.

He wondered then, whether to give Lucy Shalless the benefit of the doubt in believing that she had killed this Arispe not to save herself but so that she could take out from Vicente's now deserted camp and save whoever was to deliver the ransom.

But if there was doubt in Phil's mind about Lucy's motives, there could be no such thoughts concerning Maria! Twice she had ridden his back-trail and twice her Sharp's gun and steady finger had saved his life.

Crockett's smile thinned and died away as he recalled the still, pale face of the Spanish girl, so slim-looking in her boy's clothes, as she had lain there last night scarcely breathing under the starry sky...

The faintest flicker of movement caught his eye, breaking into his thoughts and causing him to slide the carbine slowly forward, careful to keep the barrel down, away from the sun's rays.

He saw the tip of a dust-covered stetson beyond an outcrop of rock nearly a hundred yards away. He waited breathlessly, watching carefully as the man's head and shoulders gradually came into view.

There was a wariness about this man who had approached so silently. Even now he was not prepared to offer himself to view or as a likely target, but remained squatted down on his bootheels, head turning from side to side in a wide covering sweep, while his black eyes studied the terrain surrounding Mesa Rock and the trail leading up to the mountains. Across his knees he held a carbine, his right hand on the stock, over the breech.

From his vantage point, Crockett's eyes narrowed and filled with hate as he identified the cautious man as Web Skogee!

The coyote has returned to feast on the spoils left by his dead masters!

Skogee remained hunkered down searching with his eyes narrowed against heat and glare. The wound in his left arm, though only slight, was like a nagging toothache, and the sweat pouring into it was not helping to close up the flesh where Esteban's wildly fired bullet had seared the lawman's arm.

Yesterday, he had made good his escape, taking both his own horse and the dead Frank Peck's. For Skogee had little doubt that the sheriff had been killed by that lung-piercing bullet he had fired at such easy range.

Afterwards, the deputy had found a natural hide-out some four-five miles from the spot and had holed up, wolfing down the remains of the food in the two saddle-bags and tending to the bloody flesh wound as well as possible.

The two things that gave Skogee cause for most concern, over and above the consideration of grabbing the dinero, was the lack of water and lack of feed for the horses. But the strain of long, hard riding and many hours in the fierce sun, coupled with his wound, was beginning to tell.

By night, Skogee had done all he could for the time being. The horses were carefully hobbled, the evening meal had been eaten and his wounded arm bandaged. The fatigue of sheer exhaustion crept over him like a warm all enveloping blanket and, tough as he was, Skogee had had to give way...

He had slept long and peacefully and had awakened hungry and thirsty and with his arm no more than a little painful and stiff. He could still use his carbine or six-gun if need be. He grinned wolfishly at the thought as he drank the last of the canteen water and tightened his belt against that moment later in the day when he would find plenty of grub and water at Vicente's camp twenty miles into the mountains.

Skogee saddled his own horse and, after checking his guns, swung up into leather, thinking about the chore ahead. It was unlikely that even Esteban would have been able to follow his tracks across this arid, boulder-slashed country on the fringe of the foothills. Thus, Web was not unduly worried that his position would be known or his camp discovered. He thought with grim humour on the scene of slaughter as he had last seen it. Crockett had gone down, either dead or wounded; the other slim, dark-clad rider whom Skogee had immediately recognized and had shot – Maria – was almost certainly dead, or else, like Crockett, well out of the picture! Vicente was also buzzard meat and the other two, whom Web had identified in spite of black bandanas, Ramirez and Pedro had both gone to join their master!

That only left the Shalless girl and possibly one other of Vicente's band at the camp!

Again Skogee grinned as he thought how easy it would be to handle them!

But a wariness came into the man as he neared Mesa Rock. He didn't know as yet whether Crockett, Esteban and the rest would still be there. But the way he figured it was that the mozo would have immediately ridden for help and, by this time, the place should be clear of interfering bustards! Had Esteban thought to take the ransom money back or had he, in his haste and urgency to get the dead and wounded back to town, forgotten that sack lying at the foot of Mesa Rock?

That was the question which had burned in Skogee's brain since awakening this morning. A bird in the hand might be worth a sight more than several birds in Vicente's camp, *if he were unable to locate the cache!*

Now, leaving his horse ground-anchored in a thick clump of high brush, Skogee began his careful advance and survey of the scene.

Once, indeed, the thought of a trap flashed into his mind. The country here, almost any part of it, was ideal for ambush. Supposing the money *were* there and he came forward to grab it, giving some bushwhacker his long-awaited chance?

Skogee examined the possibility and found it so full of holes he actually laughed.

Peck was either dead or badly wounded and wouldn't be able to do a thing for days, weeks, maybe never. The same went for Maria and although Skogee was not so sure about Crockett, he *had* seen him stretched out on the ground, hit by a slug from one of the Mexes' guns. As to the others, their bodies were still lying at the foot of the trail. He could see their shapes even from here, dark against the yellow and dun-coloured rocks.

That left only Esteban and, by God! he'd be too damned busy with his load of cripples to think of anything but getting them back to town!

Skogee grinned and wiped his face as he squatted on the rocks, carbine across his knees. He had stayed that way for nearly a half-hour, until his leg muscles began to ache. And during that time nothing, he swore, had moved or betrayed any sign of life save the big red-necked birds of prey circling lower and lower over three corpses.

One question Skogee should have asked

himself. *Why didn't the buzzards descend at once to their gruesome repast?*

He stood up now, ready to fling himself forward and down at the slightest hint of danger. If a bushwhacker's bullet were coming his way, it would come now. That was what Skogee figured, and, again, he was wrong!

He came forward from the rocks openly now, yet still guarded in his actions to the extent of holding his carbine ready and sweeping the immediate vicinity with his bright glance.

The sun was not yet quite overhead and the money sack lay bulging and inviting in the narrow arc of shadow thrown from Mesa Rock.

He paused only for a few seconds to glance around once again, his gaze moving briefly over the dead Mexicans, his presence sending the carrion birds to wheel or perch higher up the towering walls.

Then Skogee, knowing that the sack was fairly heavy, transferred the carbine to his damaged arm and grasped the spoils in his right hand with a grunt of satisfaction, which was cut short by the cold voice speaking behind him.

CHAPTER 17

'ONE LAST CHORE!'

'Drop it, Skogee! *Drop it I say,* or by God I'll blow you apart right where you are!'

Web Skogee's eyes turned as black as a diamond-back's. He knew that voice and wondered, with rising fury, how it was that Crockett could have stayed behind, wounded, and waiting all this time in the burning sun.

He heard the sharp metallic sound of a shell being levered into a breech and quickly dropped both sack and carbine, lifting his hands up to shoulder level and turning slowly, cautiously to gaze into the hated face of the man who had baulked him and humiliated him at every move.

'I'm going to give you a chance that you wouldn't be crazy enough to give any man yourself, Skogee,' Phil said between tight lips.

The deputy's eyes narrowed to hide the glint of triumph as he watched the fool army man carefully lower the hammer of the cocked Winchester and place the weapon at his feet.

But all the while Crockett's hard gaze was

riveted on that red, glistening face in front of him. He felt a raw upsurge of angry hate against this renegade who, hiding behind a law-badge, had murdered either directly or indirectly, Cass Cherry and the other two troopers in the first hold-up. Crockett was remembering, too, that Corporal Fellows and Trooper Jones had died during that second ambush at Hondo Bend, and that since then, this man in front of him had deliberately shot down Frank Peck and had hit Maria badly. Perhaps she would not live, Phil thought, or perhaps she would remain a cripple all her life! Sweat stood out on Crockett's lean, stubbled jaw. His eyes glittered with the dark fury of his feelings.

His voice came out to the watching lawman, harsh and cracked. 'I'm giving you this chance, Skogee, dam' your eyes to hell! You got a gun, then reach for it pronto!'

Before even Phil's words were lost on the air, Web Skogee's hand had dropped with the speed of a hawk in flight. His gun was half clear of leather before Phil's hand closed over the butt of the Walker Colt, forefinger threading the trigger, thumb hauling back on the hammer with urgent, violent speed.

Skogee's gun roared a fraction of a second before Crockett's and Phil was never nearer death as the bullet ploughed a course high up between his left arm outflung and his side. As it was, the shock of that burn almost spoiled his aim, but the hammer was already striking and the bullet speeding from the barrel as Phil staggered slightly on his wounded leg.

Crockett's brain raced in a streak of ice-cold reaction as he drew back the hammer for a second shot. A second shot that wasn't necessary and would never be discharged!

He watched the double-crossing lawman fold up slowly, his big frame seemingly loath to keel over or his legs to give way.

He even triggered another shot as he gradually fell, but the bullet only ploughed a ragged course through the sand and rocks at his feet.

He crashed full length, sending up a small dust cloud and Crockett, lean and tense and ready, watched Web Skogee die and join the other renegades, out there at Mesa Rock under the hot noon sun...

He stood awhile, gazing almost vacantly at the still figure so grotesquely sprawled, one leg bent under him. The buzzards flapped their wings with obscene impatience and put their beady gazes to the scene below.

Slowly, Crockett sheathed his smoking gun and as slowly, reached forward to retrieve the five thousand dollars ransom money which, in his greediness, Skogee had been unable to resist trying to grab.

There was nothing Phil could do about the body. The gelding could not be expected to make a quick return to Hondo Bend with a double load. Crockett viewed the decision with a complete lack of emotion. Skogee, like his Mex compadres, had been a coyote. Let him die like one out here in this arid country.

Suddenly he felt physically and mentally weary. The reaction to the strain of the last twenty-four hours was beginning to make itself felt. He started to push his tired body away from the area of so much bitter fighting and, hefting the sack and the carbine, one in each hand, limped and stumbled his way back to the hidden gelding...

It was morning by the time Crockett reached Hondo Bend. A weary, swaying, dust-covered figure with a sack of money across the faltering gelding's withers and a dazed look in his eyes.

Holt Caddo and Seward Shalless caught his reeling body as he half fell from leather. Jeff, on a sudden hunch at the sound of hoofs, ran out from the cantiña, to the board-walk. There was only a scattering of interested spectators at this early hour and they watched as the barkeep motioned for Crockett to be helped inside El Cuchillo.

Jeff caught up the sack, while Seward Shalless, betraying an unusual and unexpected strength, helped the alcalde to lead the wounded man inside and upstairs.

They laid him on the bed, removing his

boots, while Jeff hovered anxiously in the background.

Once, Crockett opened his tightly-closed eyes and moved his dust-caked lips.

'Sleep,' he mumbled and drifted off into the heaven of complete and utter oblivion...

It was lamplight time when Crockett stirred and opened his eyes, squinting at first against the strong yellow lights in his room.

Someone arose from the shadows beyond, taking the lamp next to Crockett's cot and moving it away a little distance.

He saw now that there were two men in the room. Jeff, the barkeep, his face screwed up anxiously, and the doctor hombre – what was his name? – yes, Doc Treybor.

Crockett, feeling wonderfully refreshed, struggled to a sitting position, hunching his shoulders against the pillows at his back.

'How the heck long have I been sleeping?' he asked Jeff. 'Hell! It must've been all day!'

Jeff grinned now, seeing that the army man was more his old self, and Doc Treybor moved into the circle of light, gazing down at his patient with evident satisfaction.

'All day, Crockett?' he smiled. 'You came in early Friday morning and slept and slept and slept! It's now *Saturday* evening–'

'Hell!' Crockett exploded, making a move to leap out of bed only to be checked by the sudden pain in his leg. 'Why didn't someone tell me?' he finished with a gasp.

'What's the hurry, Pete?' Jeff smiled. 'You ain't figurin' on goin' someplace are you?'

'If he is,' Treybor cut in severely, 'he'd better think again. You've slept the sleep of complete exhaustion, Crockett, which has given me a chance to clean your wound properly and stitch it up. You stay right there in bed for another two-three days and I'll think of letting you get up then!'

Crockett blinked and stroked his bearded jaw. The sound was like a buzz-saw going at full tilt.

'You want a wash and shave and then plenty of hot grub,' Jeff suggested, 'but how's about a drink first?'

Crockett nodded, turning to the doctor quickly now that his scattered thoughts were more under control.

'How is Maria?' He waited breathlessly for the doctor's answer and relief bubbled in him like a fresh sprung mountain stream, cool, invigorating and fast-moving.

'She's been as near death as most folks could go and still live,' Treybor smiled, 'but she's going to be all right, I guess—'

'Is it possible for me to see her, Doc?' Phil asked with a sudden pounding of his heart.

'I'll even *order* you to, Lieutenant,' the medico said, catching up his bag from a chair, 'considering that all through her delirium, Miss Cordoba has been screaming

for "Pheel," "Pete," "Señor Crockett"!'
Treybor smiled. 'I guess all those folks are
you, and when I said not to get up, this is
the one exception I'll allow you.' He turned
with his hand on the door. 'But you haven't
washed or shaved or eaten in two days. I'd
advise you to let Jeff see to that first!'

He closed the door gently and for the first
time in many a day, Crockett laughed and
felt good.

'I'll go get some hot water and a razor,
Lieutenant,' Jeff said, involuntarily wiping
his hand on his apron front. 'Then I guess
you could go some hot tamales, frijoles,
tortillas–'

'Don't say any more, Jeff,' Crockett
begged. 'I reckon I'm plumb near starving
to death as it is!'

The barkeep nodded and moved towards
the door as Crockett called sharply to him.

'Just one thing, Jeff. Cut this lieutenant
stuff, will you? My amigos call me Phil!'

Crockett felt even better by the time he
had washed up and shaved and had wolfed
the huge plate of spiced Mex food which
Esteban had brought.

The little mozo was grinning all over his
ugly face as he handed Phil the clothes
which had been cleaned and pressed.

'You wanta see the señorita, si?' he asked.
'Maria 'as been ask for you for ver' long
time–'

'Just as soon as I get into these duds,' Crockett replied. But the task was not so easy and rather than have the mozo see him wince, Phil sent him from the room.

He struggled into pants and shirt, slowly and painfully and finally pushed his feet into the Justin boots. He stood up, swaying a little at first and limped painfully towards the wall mirror.

He was knotting the freshly pressed barcelona when a knock sounded at the door.

Crockett pulled the bandana round and with a final glance at his changed appearance limped to the door. He had been expecting Esteban, but it was Lucy Shalless who stood there timidity and defiance warring expressions on her face.

Crockett's first reaction was, *My God, but you're beautiful!* Then, strangely the warmth went out of him, leaving him as emotionless as when he had left Web Skogee to the buzzards and coyotes.

She smiled at Crockett, stepping through the doorway so that Phil was forced to give ground.

'Please forgive me for coming to see you like this, Phil,' Lucy said earnestly, 'but I had to see for myself that you were all right.'

She seated herself in the extra chair, motioning Phil to take the other one. He saw that her face was soft and smooth and rose tinted as before; her cornsilk hair glistened in the lamplight. There was no resemblance to the white-faced, dishevelled girl who had ridden out from Vicente's lair with a smoking gun in her hand, leaving behind the man she had killed.

Crockett drew out the makings, waiting for this girl to say her piece. He only smiled encouragingly as a teacher might to an earnest scholar.

'I ... I don't quite know how to begin, Phil,' she said haltingly, her full red lips trembling a little. 'My father and I have been so wrong, misjudging you in everything you did, seeing wrong in it where no wrong existed. It was the others against whom we should have directed our dislike and hatred for the things they did. Vicente and his band, Web Skogee...'

Crockett blew smoke and waved his hand as her words trailed away. His action and the cool smile implied that the thing was scarcely worth thinking about.

'It's so much water down the river, Miss Shalless. Why worry about what has happened?'

'Because until the past has been put right we cannot begin to think of the future!'

Crockett stared hard. He even forgot the quirly between his fingers. Could she mean...? No! He must be wrong!

He searched her face and saw the soft light in her dewy eyes, the pulse throbbing in her creamy neck and the invitation on her red, parted lips.

Disgust, anger, contempt, swept through him, so that he lowered his eyes to mask his feelings from this fantastic woman.

He was silent a long time, so long that the girl arose and came across to stand by his chair. Her perfume came down to him, heady like the perfume of flowering sage at dawn.

And because he felt oddly awkward at sitting, he climbed carefully to his feet and stood towering above her, looking down into the pleading upturned face.

She picked a wrong one in Skogee and now she's ready to forgive and forget, was Crockett's bleak thought.

She must have seen the hardness in his eyes then, for somehow, in some illusive way, she withdrew suddenly into herself.

The lips were as red and full as before, but the invitation was no longer there. The eyes sparkled but with the glitter of defeat rather than triumph.

'I haven't properly thanked you for all you did, Mr. Crockett,' she said, stepping back a little, 'but believe me when I saw–'

'Save it, Lucy,' Phil said. This time his old smile returned without the bitterness, without the disgust he had previously felt. He realized for perhaps the first time since meeting her that Lucy Shalless was really a

253

small girl, with a woman's shape and maturity...

Holt Caddo, the alcalde, buttonholed Crockett at the bar. Phil was looking for Esteban to guide him to Maria's room, but the bar was thronged tonight and the alcalde wiped his longhorn moustaches and gripped Crockett in triumph with the air of a conjuror producing a rabbit from a hat.

'Fill them up, Jeff,' Caddo ordered and said, turning back to Crockett, 'It's good to see you in one piece again, Lieutenant. When we toted you in here Friday morning you sure looked more dead than alive!'

Phil grinned and then, because he had had so little opportunity until then, and also because his whole being had been filled with concern for Maria, he asked the alcalde about Frank Peck.

'Frank's going to be out of his office chair for a month or more,' Holt Caddo said. 'Skogee's bullet grazed a lung. He was in pretty bad shape, too, when Bellenger and Esteban got back. Hell! Crockett, it was sure a shock even for Hondo Bend...'

Crockett nodded and let the slightly pompous Caddo prattle on. He was greatly relieved to learn that Peck was not going to die.

Phil rolled and lit another cigarette, seeking a way of escape from the mayor and the press of back-slapping customers, who fiercely insisted on refilling his glass every five minutes by the clock.

It was a little after nine when Esteban appeared, brightening at sight of Crockett at the bar and leading the willing lieutenant away from the crowd of well-wishers who had still not yet heard sufficient details of the fighting at Mesa Rock to satisfy their sharp appetites.

Esteban led the way along a lamp-lit gallery to the door of a room. He knocked and gently pushed open the door, motioning Crockett inside. Phil heard the mozo's quiet retreat behind him as he stepped forward to the big, canopied bed, limping slightly and then smiling down at the pale, beautiful face of Maria Cordoba. Her gaze reached up to his face and clung there. He read into those violet-blue eyes, bewilderment, doubt and a wild surging relief. Something inside of him stopped for a moment. It was like taking a fall from a great height and waiting for the sickening impact of the hard ground.

But the impact was not quite the same and, therefore, the analogy was not strictly correct. He sat down on the chair at her bedside, his eyes moving over her face and the black lustrous hair cascading over the white pillow.

'How does it go, Maria?' he said presently.

His voice was low and husky and sounded strange to his own ears. The red lips parted then in a smile of tenderness and a fleeting, wistful expression chased across her eyes and was gone.

'Eet ees well, Pheel, thanks to you an' Esteban an' Charles Treybor. They say I weel leeve an' be well soon. But you were wounded, señor! I saw you leemping again?'

Crockett grinned. 'I seem to be have taken enough lead recently to last most men a lifetime, but I am glad you are going to be all right, Maria.'

He leaned forward and covered her hand with his own. He told her then, quietly, so as not to excite her, all that had happened since Skogee's bullet had laid her low. Some of it she had heard from Esteban, but she pressed Crockett for all the details and then lay back, strangely content to listen to the sound of his low quiet voice.

She was sleeping peacefuly again when Seguina, the Mex woman, came in softly and nodded reassuringly to the tall Americano.

Sequina stood just inside the door and Crockett, on a sudden impulse, leaned over Maria, brushing her forehead lightly with his lips.

'One last chore, Maria, and then I'll be back again,' he murmured to the sleeping girl…

CHAPTER 18

MAJOR MITCHELL SENDS WORD

Crockett found Esteban waiting in the lamplit corridor and motioned him to follow.

He led the way downstairs into Maria's parlour and there told the mozo what he intended doing.

'But you are not so well to ride, Señor Crockett,' Esteban protested. 'Thees doctor, 'e say for you to rest. 'E tell me to see that you do thees–'

Crockett made an impatient gesture with his arm. 'Treybor fusses overmuch, Esteban; so long as I go carefully it will be all right. He's stitched up my leg and the crease on my head is almost healed. Let's quit yapping and get down to business!'

The little Mex could see that the Americano lieutenant was obdurate. He shrugged and sighed expressively, rolling his black eyes up to heaven. 'You are ze boss, señor, goddam you are! You want for me to saddle 'osses an' pack food?'

Crockett nodded. 'Three saddlers and a pack-horse, Esteban. Can you meet me out front in a half-hour?'

The mozo nodded. 'I tell Jeff, then I get thees theengs ready pronto.'

Crockett ate a quick meal in the cantiña's dining-room and then unobtrusively came out onto the night-shadowed board-walk, buckling on his gun-belt.

The horses were ready and waiting, reins hitched to the rack. Crockett built and fired a smoke and before it was half-way through, Esteban appeared in bolero, concho-studded chaps and spurred riding boots. He wore the inevitable bandana around his grizzled head.

Phil nodded and both men mounted; Crockett carefully stepping into the saddle of the now rested gelding, Esteban vaulting into his own Mex-rigged kak and grasping the long lead reins of the pack-horse and spare saddler. He waited for Crockett to take the lead and followed in the gelding's dust, turning sharply down a side street and coming soon to another corner and to a group of small 'dobe and tarpaper shacks.

Esteban tied reins to a solitary post and stood a little to one side, hand on the butt of his gun as Crockett knocked sharply on the door.

A chair scraped somewhere in the shack and footsteps sounded and then stopped abruptly. The door opened a few inches and a smallish, leather-faced 'Breed looked out, sudden alarm flickering in his dark shifting eyes at sight of the two shadowy figures.

He made to slam the door but Crockett had shoved the toe of his boot between the door and lintel. He pushed hard and the door slammed back, half staggering the 'Breed back into the room.

Esteban drew his long knife, running a thumb lightly along the razor edge and testing the sharp point. His glance was black and wicked and fixed on the 'Breed's staring eyes.

'You take us quickly to Vicente's camp,' Esteban said, speaking fast in Spanish, 'else the Gringo will order me to cut out your lights and eat them for supper!' Esteban flourished the naked knife as he spoke and fear crawled over the other's face turning it the colour of a dirty saddle-blanket.

He went through the motions of expostulation; innocence and outraged indignation, but they were all half-hearted efforts. Crockett said, speaking in the tongue, 'We haven't time to waste, hombre! Better move fast if you want to live and see tomorrow's sun!'

Within ten minutes they were in the saddle. The 'Breed, who had reluctantly given his name as Yuma Jack, riding the spare saddler.

Esteban watched him like a hawk and anchored him as it were by tying the pack-horse's lead rein to Yuma Jack's saddle. That way, the 'Breed could hardly make a bolt for it, and as he was unarmed, there was nothing he could do except obey orders.

They rode until midnight and, with Esteban watching, Crockett was able to sleep until just before dawn. Breakfast was a welcome beginning to the hard day ahead and noon found them someway along the mountain trail beyond Mesa Rock.

They stopped for ten-fifteen minutes in every hour to blow the horses and now Esteban really rode hard on Yuma Jack, promising him a horrible death if he dared lead the Americano soldado along the wrong trails.

But, by this time, Yuma Jack had given up any thought of a double-cross or trying any tricks. The odds were too heavy against. He knew also from the news running around Hondo Bend that Vicente and his band were dead, as likewise the deputy, Web Skogee, whom he had feared almost as much as Vicente Tularez. He had nothing to fear from these dead men, therefore, he considered philosophically, it behoved him to obey the commands of his present masters.

Esteban, watching him closely, and perhaps understanding the workings of his simple mind, was satisfied that he would not try any tricks.

They soon reached a point beyond which Esteban was lost and now they relied entirely on Yuma Jack to lead them from one timbered bench upwards to another. The 'Breed found trails that even Esteban's eyes sometimes missed as pine stands thinned, giving way to tortuous rim-rock paths.

The afternoon sun beat down from a cloudless sky, but here, a third of the way up the Eagle Tails, the breeze was cool and fanned their burning cheeks with its refreshing touch.

Suddenly the thin trail widened out into a grassy park. So unexpected was this that Crockett drew rein and put his questioning glance over the huge stretch of grassland ahead. He knew without the telling that this was, or had been, Vicente's permanent camp and he quickly realized why.

There was everything here. Fresh mountain streams, even a small lake, and across the sun-cured mountain grass, horses and cattle grazed, corralled in safety and freedom by the very nature of the steeply rising walls on all sides.

Near to a stand of firs were a couple of rudely built cabins and scattered around in profusion and chaotic disorder was equipment of every kind. Saddles, bridles, reins, blankets, cooking utensils, including the remains of food which had already been devoured by some wild animal – even a few guns and knives as well as articles of clothing, were found scattered about. Near to the entrance to one of the huts was the stiff body of Arispe. It was a horrible sight and ants as well as buzzards had been at work.

'Get Yuma to dig a grave, Esteban,' Crockett said, turning away, sickened by the sight of the man whom Lucy had shot.

The mozo nodded and spoke his rapid order to Yuma Jack, who shrugged and seemed almost grateful for being given a task with which to occupy himself.

'Onlee one hour to sundown, Señor Crockett,' Esteban said presently, glancing at the sky. 'Pairhaps we cook some food an' begeen our search tomorrow?'

'Sure,' Crockett said, building himself a smoke. 'See if you can rustle something from the cabins – preferably something that isn't swarming with insects!'

Esteban nodded and disappeared. The mounts were safely hobbled and there was no chance of Yuma Jack making an escape, even on one of the loose, grazing horses.

They ate ravenously enough. It was a good meal and there was plenty of it, their own rations being augmented by Vicente's plentiful stocks.

This time Crockett insisted on taking over guard duty. He had had plenty of sleep of late as he explained to Esteban, and whilst it was unlikely they would be disturbed, it was just as well to be prepared...

At dawn, after an uneventful night, Crockett rolled in his blankets, sleeping deeply until nearly noon. Across from him a camp fire burned merrily, the stew-pot atop, throwing out an appetizingly savoury smell.

He sat up as Esteban fairly hurled himself from the shadow of the firs near the huts.

'We 'ave found eet, señor! We 'ave found zees cache of stolen dinero! Eet was Yuma – but I get too excited,' he grinned as he reached the fire and squatted down on bootheels to catch his breath.

Crockett grinned his pleasure and relief. *This was the end of the chapter,* he thought, *or almost.*

'How did you manage it?' he asked the mozo.

Esteban looked wise all of a sudden. 'We start in thees morneeng, airly, an' I say to Yuma, look you goddam sonofabeetch, zees two rancherias, zees huts, one she ees beeg an' one she ees small!

'Yuma look blank, like you say eembeeceel, but I say zees small one ees where Vicente an' his lieutenant sleep. Zere are signs scattered about to prove eet!'

'So?' Phil smiled.

'So we do not bot'er weeth zees beeg hut, but go to work dam' queeck in ze small one. We rip up zee boards an' after an hour, mebbe two, behold! We find mucho dinero, een sacks an' boxes–'

'How did you figure out to start looking where you did, Esteban?' Phil interrupted.

The mozo then told how he had tried to figure the thing out from Vicente's point of view. No doubt there were a million caves and crevices in the surrounding walls where a man might safely hide a fortune, but Vicente had a large following of cut-throats, murderers and robbers. He would not trust his haul out of sight, of reach, once he had apportioned the men their agreed share of the spoils!

Crockett nodded in admiration of Esteban's reasoning.

'So,' Esteban said, 'eet was not too deeficult to imagine zat zee 'uts zemselves might be a likely 'iding place!

'We were goddam lucky, I guess,' Esteban finished modestly. 'Now Yuma, 'e put ze dinero een sacks we tote on ze pack-hoss...'

On the outskirts of Hondo Bend, the dust-covered riders halted at a sign from Crockett.

He turned to the thoroughly subdued 'Breed, 'I don't know how deep you were in this, Yuma, maybe not too deep, but you've committed a crime against the territory and the army as well–'

Yuma Jack turned pleading eyes towards the Americano. 'Plees, señor, I do nozing except ride weeth ze meesages, but eef you

264

weel let me, I weel get a job pronto, tomorrow, even today…'

Crockett turned away to hide a smile, wondering whether or not he were dealing too leniently with the man. Still, he had led them to Vicente's camp – probably the only man in the district who could have done – and, as far as Crockett knew, he had not really committed any crimes.

Phil said, 'You do that, Yuma, get a job and keep your nose clean, you sabe?'

The man's thanks were profuse, suggesting by that very fact, that he was more guilty than he appeared. But, hell! Crockett shrugged and told the 'Breed to beat it. They watched as he went on his way, flourishing his sombrero and turning in the saddle to wave his arm.

As they walked their horses down Main, a rider exploded into view from the other end of the street, hauling up at the rack fronting El Cuchillo in a cloud of dust.

Crockett spurred forward, a grin of recognition spreading across his dust-caked lips at sight of the black-bearded top sergeant of 'C' Troop.

'You habla weet' the soldado, señor,' Esteban said, coming up behind Crockett. 'I weel look after thees dinero!'

Crockett nodded and swung from leather. Bryne Ewart had turned on the board-walk at the sound of pounding hoofs, and now stood to attention, his wild black face and blue eyes alight with pleasure.

'At ease, Sergeant,' Phil said swinging onto the walk after briefly returning the sergeant's salute. 'What news?'

''Tis the major himself who is sending good news for you, sir,' Ewart said. 'A week's leave before you need report back for duty. It's all here, sir, in this letter,' the sergeant continued, removing his gauntlet and thrusting a hand inside his tunic.

He passed over the letter, adding, 'Lieutenant Martin made his report, sir, and later, the major called me in for this courier job, to check on whether you were all right and to deliver this letter.'

Phil nodded, slitting the envelope with his knife and quickly perusing Major Blaine Mitchell's precise copperplate. There was quite a screed about Giff Martin's interim report on the hold-up at Hondo Bend and an order to give Sergeant Ewart a brief but concise written report on the happenings subsequent to the fight at the Hondo.

'I'll write out a report for you to take back, Bryne,' Crockett grinned. 'Right now I've got a couple of calls to make. Do you think you could kill a little time at the bar in El Cuchillo?'

Sergeant Bryne Ewart's face positively glowed. 'The lieutenant wouldn't be jokin', would he, sir?'

Crockett grinned and shook his head and Ewart, with a casual but wholly adequate and correct salute, turned towards the batwing doors...

Doctor Charles Treybor looked up from his desk as the 'patient' was shown in.

'Is your leg troubling you, Crockett? If so you'd better let me–'

But the lieutenant was shaking his head and smiling. 'Nothing like that is troubling me, Doc, though I'm sure sorry I had to go riding against your orders. There was something I had to do–'

Treybor nodded. 'I was an army medico once, Crockett. I guess I know how it is.'

'Listen,' Phil said, leaning his sun-blackened hands on the doctor's table. 'How soon will it be before Maria Cordoba is able to be up and about?'

Treybor pulled at his lower lip and gazed shrewdly up at the lieutenant from underneath his grey eyebrows. 'I guess you've got an almighty good reason for asking, Lieutenant,' he replied presently. 'How long do you want me to say? A month? A fortnight? A week?'

Crockett flushed slightly. 'I have a week's leave from the fort,' he began, 'I was wondering–'

Treybor nodded slowly. This time it was his turn to smile. 'I think it would do her

267

good, just so long as you are careful, Lieutenant, but no honeymooning away from Hondo Bend; not at present. I want you both right here where I can keep my eyes on you. That is an order. Is it understood?'

'Perfectly, Doc,' Phil returned grinning and straightening up. 'You have my word on that.'

Crockett was back at El Cuchillo in the space of minutes, ascending the stairs and making for the door along the corridor. He knocked gently and Maria's soft voice told him 'come in.' He crossed the room and stood looking down at her, taking in the breathless beauty, absorbing the glad welcome in her violet-blue eyes.

Briefly he told her of their trip to Vicente's camp; the recovery of the money, including most of that looted from the army pay-wagon as well as the money stolen from Hondo Bend's bank.

Maria listened gravely until he had finished, her eyes now sombre and fixed intently on his face as though she would permanently record every feature, every plane of light and shadow in the recesses of her mind.

'You go back now to thee fort, Pheel?' she said, when he had finished. It was more a statement than a question.

He sat down then on the chair beside her bed and took her hand between his own.

268

'I've got a week's leave,' he smiled. 'Sergeant Ewart, that damned Irish trooper, has just ridden in.'

'What weel you do, Pheel? Weet' your week, I mean?' There was the barest tremor in her voice. She was looking across the room so that he would not see what was in her eyes.

Crockett's voice was so low and soft that the two of them were in a small, secure world of their own.

'I have also just seen the doc, Maria. He said that it would do you no harm to be up within a week – just to be married – and just so long as we both spend the time right here in town!'

There was a shining radiant quality in her eyes now as she turned them to Crockett's dark face, bent close to hers.

'What are you trying to say, Pheel?'

'Only this, querida, that I love you so much I would be eternally grateful if you would do me the honour of marrying me?' The words might have sounded high-toned but there was nothing in Crockett's heart beyond sincerity and a deep abiding love.

She lifted tear-stained eyes to his face and put out her hand to touch his stubbled, dusty jaw.

But the smile was not far in back of those glistening eyes and when she said, 'Kees me, Pheel,' it had reached her trembling lips...

269

The publishers hope that this book has given you enjoyable reading. Large Print Books are especially designed to be as easy to see and hold as possible. If you wish a complete list of our books please ask at your local library or write directly to:

Dales Large Print Books
Magna House, Long Preston,
Skipton, North Yorkshire.
BD23 4ND